SEEKERS

Seekers

A novel

DAVID FUNG

Lit Magic Publishing

Montreal, Quebec

Fung, David 1982–

Seekers

Book cover design by Lit Magic Publishing

Park illustration by Michael Rehder

Typeset in Adobe Caslon Pro

ISBN: 978-1-9990287-3-2

10 9 8 7 6 5 4 3 2 1

For Mama and Papa

Park Illustration

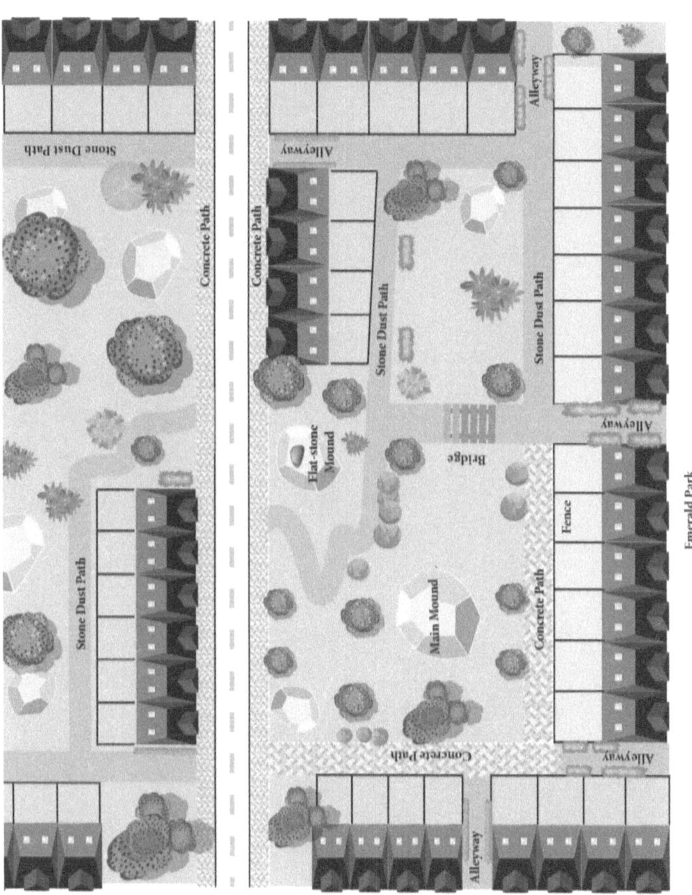

1

The leaves are stirring. Someone's hiding behind them, but I can't say who. The bushes are so thick I can't see through them; I can't see anyone at all. At least I won't be running much 'cause the bushes are close to the ball. I hope I win today. When we play kick-the-can I'm almost always the seeker, but every time I'm it I never win. Sometimes I want to scream *I'm leaving! I quit!* and go home, or kick the ball real far, then run away so they would all be hiding for nothing. I wish I were bigger and faster, with superpowers so no one would beat me. So I would win.

The game has started, and I have no captives yet. I head over to the bushes. There's someone there—I can feel it. I'm scared of parting the leaves, so I walk slowly around the bushes, and that's when I catch something, a flash of blue between the leaves. Curly hair, too. Brown, very short. And now a face appears, showing green eyes. I run as fast as I can. I run to the soccer ball, not looking back.

"Rex!" I yell, stepping on the ball. "Rex, I found you! You're hiding in the bushes!"

Rex comes out of the bushes, angry-looking, and spits on the grass. I wander off to the next hideout: the little bridge over there, beyond the bushes. If I want to, I can check those pine trees at the other end, but they're just too far away from the ball. The alleyways are the best hideouts, and the park has five of them. Three are not too far, while the other two are behind the bridge, each in a corner. I focus my attention on the bridge, listening, hoping to see a part of Hank or Finn that'll give them away.

Even with the sun heading down the air is hot. Barbecues are in full swing. Doors are opening and closing. Neighbours are sitting on their balconies, reading a book, spying on each other, enjoying what's left of the afternoon sun. Someone's giggling; it's either Lacey or Cara hiding in an alleyway.

"Quit hugging the ball!" Rex says.

"I'm not hugging it."

"Get off the mound, Red. Move!"

"No," I tell him. "You're not my boss."

I'm not sure what to do. I look around, still standing on the main mound[1], not far from Rex (his eyes seem to be staring at the bridge), and suddenly I hear noise coming from the alleyway closest to me. I walk down the main mound, down to where the alleyway is, feeling my heart beat faster and faster. Who's there? I ask myself. Who? Someone's running. I turn around and see that it's Aaron. He's younger, only six, but I'm eight, and I can outrun him. I step on the ball and call him out seconds before he reaches it. I start back down the mound,

––––––

1. The mound where the soccer ball must be during a game of kick-the-can.

looking at the bridge just in case, at the pine trees and other hideouts farther out behind the bridge.

And now I'm close. Very close to the alleyway. I'm trying to pick up sounds of movement in the bushes, but it's hard to concentrate when the neighbours to my left are chatting and laughing. Carefully, without waiting any longer, I enter the alleyway. The bushes on the right-hand side have gaps near the ground. I crouch and check for skin, for shoes, but nothing's there. I go over to the bushes on the left-hand side, and that's when I spot Lacey. She's looking straight at me, and I'm looking down at her brown eyes and little mouth through the gaps between the leaves. There's another face, too, beside hers. The hair isn't brown like Lacey's but yellow. And only Cara has yellow hair. Cara's not looking at me, but I'm looking at her and I run; I run back up the mound and step on the ball.

"Cara and Lacey, come out! You're in the alleyway!"

I wait awhile. They don't come out.

"Cara, Lacey, come out!"

I yell out their names one more time, and only then do they come out. Lacey's skipping with her head down, skipping up the mound toward me, while Cara's walking slowly, giving me one of her hard looks. For some strange reason Cara doesn't seem to like me that much. She talks a lot to Lacey, and they're always together. In a way I wish I were Cara—only *sometimes*—'cause then I'd be Lacey's best friend and I'd care for her just like I care for my toys; I'd run with her, hide with her in the bushes, behind the bridge, where I'd cover her with myself. Where I'd make her invisible so that I'd be caught and she'd be free.

"I hope we won't play another game," Lacey says, stopping next to me.

"We don't need to. We can do what we want."

"Like what?"

"We can always bike. Or we can talk on the bridge."

"That's true."

I feel good with her by my side. I feel like she's my girl-friend or something, only without the hand-holding and the kissing. I want to tell her she's pretty, prettier than Cara. I think she'd like that.

"Or maybe we can go to Mickey's later," I suggest, walking down with her to the base of the main mound.

She looks at me, thinking, and runs her hair behind her ear, looking down now, not saying anything. Her nails are light purple and sparkly, and the beads of her bracelet are blue and red and green.

"I'd have to ask him first," I tell her, "but he'll say yes, I know. We can play a board game if you want. Or watch a movie, something like that."

"I don't know," she says. "I'd have to ask my mom."

"That's okay."

She smiles and turns away, skipping in the fading light. I set off toward the flat-stone mound. Along the way I hear Aaron cry out, "Alf, hide!" For a split second I see hair behind the flat-stone mound, but is it Alf's hair? With no one coming to kick the ball, I walk up the flat-stone mound and step on the stone. There's Alf, my next captive, lying still as a statue with his face buried in the grass.

A short time later I manage to find everyone else except Hank, Finn, and Mickey. I finally reach the other side of the bridge. No one's there, so I walk on, toward the two farthest alleyways. I'm so close to winning I can't make a mistake,

I just can't. If I get too close to Hank or Finn, I'll lose for sure 'cause they're older and faster—but wait. Something's wrong… Why are they are cheering? Who's laughing? I turn around.

There's Hank and Finn on the main mound, right next to the ball. "Come and get it!" Hank shouts. But how's that possible? Someone's approaching me from behind. It's my best friend, Mickey.

"They cheated, Red. They cheated!"

"You saw them?"

"I was hiding with them," he says. "But they got tired of waiting, so they left. They're idiots, Red, you know that. I told them not to leave the park 'cause that's cheating, but they didn't listen and called me a wimp."

Me and Mickey stop on the deck of the bridge and sit on the rail. Hank and Finn aren't even looking in our direction; they're busy chatting with the captives and laughing.

"You want to hang out with Lacey? I don't feel like playing with those assholes."

"We can go to my place, then," Mickey says.

"Yeah."

"My parents won't mind. What do you want to do, though? We can't play with my figurines. I mean, she's a girl."

"I don't know. Maybe a board game?"

"Yeah, we can do that."

Hank's still waiting for me on the main mound, with the soccer ball moving back and forth under his shoe. He expects me to walk up to him, but what's the point? He'll kick the ball real hard and the game will start all over again. I'm tired of playing. I'm tired of losing and losing, always losing.

"So?" Hank says. "Aren't you coming, loser?"

"Why would I? If you're going to kick it, just kick it."

"Come on, you wuss. I don't have all day!"

"You're a cheater!" I shout.

"And you're good for nothing!"

"Kick the ball, dumb-ass!"

"What did you call me?" he asks, taking his foot off the ball. "What did you just say?"

"Come on, Hank," Rex says. "Kick the ball. I want to hide."

"Shut up, Rex, I wasn't talking to you."

"Just kick the damn ball!" I shout.

Hank finally kicks it. The ball rolls down the mound, but it doesn't stop 'cause Hank's behind it, kicking it again and again until it reaches an alleyway where he kicks it again. Everyone's waiting for me to get the ball—everyone but Mickey and Lacey. She's coming toward us. Me and Mickey get up and walk off the bridge. The three of us head to the closest alleyway and disappear in it, leaving the others without their seeker. The ball belongs to Rex, so I really don't care what happens to it.

"Where the fuck are you going?" Hank cries out. "Wuss! Come back here!"

We're out of the alleyway, out of the park, and now we're walking to Mickey's house on the same block. Mickey's parents don't like it when visitors come in from the balcony, so we have to go in from the front. But first Mickey needs to ask his parents. He goes in while me and Lacey wait outside on his front steps. Hank's mother happens to be outside, too, watering flowers and plants on her front porch two houses down. She spots me and asks me how I'm doing. Raising my voice, I say, "I'm fine, Mrs. Fields."

"How's your mother? Is she all right, too?"

"Yeah, she's okay."

"Good. That's good," she says, smiling. "Are you having fun with Hank in the park?"

"Have a great day, Mrs. Fields."

2

The old beggar sits there against the wall of a skyscraper with his grocery cart beside him, thinking about money. He plans to spend some of his coins on a doughnut, a muffin maybe, something to go with the soy milk he's saving for supper. Money. It's there, all around him. Hidden and out of reach in purses, in pockets, jingling at times, reminding him of the dollars he used to make for a living. He hasn't eaten much since he awoke this morning (just a peach given by a friendly stranger two or three days ago), and he can feel the ache throbbing in his throat, that aching need for something to quench his thirst.

The air is hotter now, the wind long gone. His hand lies outstretched on the ground next to a coffee cup scant of coins. He closes his eyes, his head tilted forward, and listens to the din he's grown so accustomed to, that conglomeration of voices unclear and distinct, of car wheels accelerating, slowing down, guitar music being played somewhere distant, hundreds of footsteps approaching all at once, hundreds moving away, fading away, laughter. He still hasn't decided whether he'll sleep in a park or under a bridge. Nor does he know if he should leave his current spot and panhandle elsewhere, like in the shade over there, under a tree. He sees three couples coming his way and makes an effort to speak.

"Spare change, please? Sir, ma'am, spare change? Spare change?"

The women pay him no mind and walk on. One of the men, however, stops in front of him and fumbles in his pocket for money. He takes out three or four coins, drops them into the beggar's cup without looking at him, and walks on. The beggar thanks him, wishes him a wonderful day, but this time the man doesn't stop; he doesn't look back.

The beggar, nodding to himself, thinks about how much more he could get before sunset. He spots Cole approaching, Cole the friendly bespectacled Samaritan, clad today in a loose blue polo shirt and black corduroy pants. He straightens himself, expecting a greeting, a bit of small talk, some change. Cole stops at arm's length from him and says, "Hot day, isn't it?"

"Sure is," the beggar says, squinting at Cole's wide-set eyes, his double chin, the plastic bag swaying gently in his hand.

"How are you holding up today?" Cole asks, crouching.

"I'm all right."

"Yeah?"

"Sure thing. I'm all right."

"Here." Cole hands him the bag. "Brought you something. It's not much, but it's always better than nothing."

The beggar takes the bag and produces from it a yellow apple, a 250 mL carton of orange juice, a box of six granola bars, and a sandwich. *Q*, he tells himself, staring at Cole. If I had to choose a letter for him, it would certainly be *Q*.

"Is that okay?"

"Oh, yes!" the beggar says, smiling like a child holding a birthday present. "Very much appreciated!"

"I don't have any change at the moment," Cole says.

"Don't worry about that. Food's always better anyway." Still, he thinks, putting each item back into the bag, still it would've been nice to have a bit of change. "Where are you off to?"

"I was thinking of going to the music store before my break ends. I've been trying to go there this week but never got around to it. Work's been hectic."

"You seem to be managing fine."

"I try to stay afloat," he says, and casts a sideways glance at the music store two streets away. "It's the summertime rush. More work. Less personnel. I guess I'll just have to tough it out like everybody else. You won't find me here in three weeks, though."

"No?"

"I'll be off on a trip for a week."

"That's great news. You've earned it, Cole. Where are you going?"

"A beach resort in Costa Rica."

"Ah, the beach. That's always good. You'll be exploring, too, I hope?"

"I'll try to, yeah."

While Cole goes on about his Costa Rica trip, the beggar can't help but conjure up waves and seashells, parasols and corrugated sand. He finds himself only half listening, not wanting to listen. Suddenly his mind transports him to a bygone time, to another place far away from the zones of his reality. There he is now, all alone and naked, in a lake. Alone and unburdened, feeling the water as he moves and the heat of the sun on his shoulders. The waves are there in the distance, approaching, massing themselves. He can picture them stroking him gently, lifting him from the sand floor and pushing him back, riding past him now, away, farther and farther away, splashing glittery blue all over the shore.

"I guess I better go," Cole says, severing the lake scene. "I should've brought some change for you. Sorry about that."

"There's nothing to apologize for," the beggar says. "Oh, I almost forgot. Did you get any news about the raise?"

"I did." Cole's eyes light up. "I got the raise. I got more than what I'd asked."

"I was hoping you'd get it."

"I was expecting the worst, but I'm glad I got it."

"I'm happy for you," the beggar says. "I truly am."

"If you want, I can stay a little longer. I can always go to the store another time."

"No, no—go to the store."

"Yeah?"

The beggar nods and says, "We'll talk again."

"You'll be here next week?"

"Right here. You can count on me."

Cole puts his hand on the beggar's shoulder. "I'll see you next week, then."

The beggar watches him rise. Smiling, without saying another word, Cole steps into the midday throng, dissolving as he walks on until he's nothing but a speck, a spot of brown glistening, shrinking, among other bobbing heads.

Once Cole's out of sight, the beggar seizes the apple in the bag and takes his first bite.

The effect is instantaneous. He opens his mouth again, bites off a chunk twice as big as his first, and now, chewing less, still savouring the sweetness of that flesh, he reaches into the bag for the juice, for more food, filling himself until only the sandwich and three granola bars remain.

3

My girlfriend's a financial analyst. She's an accomplished woman, outgoing and always outspoken, but I'm not like her. I work at a local school, as a janitor. My work doesn't pay as much as hers, that's for sure. Let's just say that without her, rent would be a problem—bar drinks and ice cream, even movie nights and the occasional takeout would no longer be an option. The worst part would be living without booze, but I don't think I ever will. I'd have to be real sick or dirt poor to give up something that good.

Speaking of booze, I'm holding a Heineken, and this one's fresh out of the fridge. It's a nice, cheerful midmorning—blue sky, scattered clouds, the sun like a blazing full moon, back from a two-day hiatus—the very first Saturday in June. With a bit of air coming in I can hear birds chirping, kids yelling, construction equipment hollering nearby, but all that noise doesn't bother me. I step away from the open balcony door and take a seat on the couch. The TV is on, showing a repeat of yesterday's match between the Red Sox and the Yankees. (Sadly the Red Sox lost by two points.)

People from everywhere have all sorts of rituals—coffee in the morning being the most common one, I guess. There's a teacher I know who does twenty sit-ups, thirty push-ups, seventy jumping jacks in his backyard every day, rain or shine. Why he tortures himself this way so often is beyond me. Another teacher lights thirty candles before taking a bath just to calm her nerves, but I honestly don't get how you can remain calm in the bathtub when your home is on fire. My ritual is simple: drinking a cold beer on the couch, watching TV, just sitting here without having to leave the apartment, without having to think about anything—now *that's* a great Saturday morning ritual. My girlfriend isn't so fond of it, though—the drinking, I mean. I try not to talk back when she complains about it. I've never been much of a talker, and I don't want to argue with anyone, yell at anyone. I much prefer silence.

"I have something planned with Sue tomorrow," Candy says.

She's sitting in one of the dining room chairs, applying some purple nail polish to her toenails. She has one leg bent like a tent in front of her, and she's leaning a bit forward so that her chin is resting on her knee. I'm observing her at an angle. I find her real pretty in that pose, with that strip of hair falling over her forehead. If I were an artist, I'd do a painting of her right then and there.

I tell her she's pretty, but she doesn't react. She doesn't make eye contact.

"What are you going to do?"

"Girl stuff," she says. "Massage. Shopping. Maybe we'll meet up with other friends. I don't know yet."

The Red Sox are leading by two points, for now. Tilting my head back, I take one, two, three sips of my beer before lowering it to a spot between my thighs.

Candy goes on: "Don't worry, though; you're not invited. But if you were, we both know you wouldn't show up anyway."

"If it's about Friday evening, I said I was sorry. It wasn't on purpose. You know that."

She looks up at me, her expression threatening. "It's never on purpose, is it? We had agreed on the time and place," she says, raising her voice. "Six p.m. Caesar's. And you forgot! I was at the restaurant, waiting for you. But you *never* came. One hour I waited, alone like a fool."

Her eyes are brimming with anger, rooting me to the couch. There was a time when I used to enjoy looking into them; from up close I used to marvel at the details I really loved, the details I was so jealous of: the rich glassy-blue colour, the fibres stretching out over the blue like tiny white roots floating on ocean water. They certainly had a way of pulling me in, of putting me under their spell. Not anymore. They're not the same as they once were. Still beautiful but less appealing to me. More insensitive over time, with every quarrel.

She looks back down at her paint job and starts purpling the nail of her little toe. "And next time," she says, "pay attention. If I say *unsweetened soy*, it's unsweetened soy, not vanilla. This isn't rocket science. I reminded you—twice! But the thing is, you don't listen, you don't care. You'd rather sit on your ass and drink yourself to death."

My eyes widen in disbelief. I'm pretty sure even to Candy this whole soy milk affair is flat-out ridiculous. Why make it sound so terrible? Why make such a big deal out of it? Because she knows I can't possibly talk back to her. How can I after Friday's episode? After she found herself waiting for me at Caesar's, waiting there for nothing, waiting all alone like a fool? To her it's beyond self-evident: I can't talk back to her, so I *have* to take the punch; I *have* to feel even more guilty, more miserable. But I won't take the punch, Candy. No. Certainly not for this stupid grocery shopping mistake.

"What's the matter with you?"

"What's the matter with *me*?" she says, taking her foot off the chair.

"Can't you say anything positive? Always accusing me of something I did or didn't do. Nothing you say about me is ever good, ever. Nothing I do is ever good enough for you."

"So now you want a compliment? Is that it?"

"When was the last time you said anything good about me? When?"

"What do you want me to say? That you're remarkable? Charming? That you're everything I wish for in a man?" she says, and lets out an irritating snicker, something she often does during an argument.

Hearing her laugh that way upsets me so much I want to hurt her. Anyone would think that pretty people are attractive, people like Candy with stunning blue eyes and full lips and perfect skin—but no. Sometimes I can't stand looking at her, listening to her voice, being in the same room with her. I think it's pretty ironic.

"No," she says, capping the nail polish bottle. "You're the problem. *You.* Even now, even after all these years, I'm still amazed I can put up with *you*—a drunk with no friends."

My eyes narrow at the sight of her heading to our bedroom with a mild smirk on her face, an air of triumph in her posture. She doesn't say anything else, and neither do I.

4

Summer is by far my favourite season. When the school year is over, me and my neighbourhood friends all meet up in Emerald Park, which we just call the park. We don't even call each other up. Some of us go to the park late in the afternoon, and then more people come out 'cause they hear us playing, and soon enough we're almost a dozen in the park. Sometimes I don't wait until late afternoon. Sometimes I call Mickey, or he calls me, and we play board games or watch movies at his house. When Mickey comes over to my place, we play with my action figurines or draw stuff, but that's about it. Mickey doesn't mind.

We're outside today, having the best time. We're biking in the street, around the block, and I'm following him. Cars are coming up from behind us but not too fast, while the wind is blowing against us, making my T-shirt stick to my skin like a second skin. Mickey slows down and eases his bike up onto the sidewalk, so I do the same. We make one complete trip around the block before Mickey enters an alleyway, and now off we go into the park. Lacey and Cara are there, on the deck of the bridge.

The path we're on continues along the length of the park, but it also branches out to where the bridge is. Mickey doesn't go to the bridge. As we pass the girls from a distance I see Lacey crouching, staring down at something. Half of me wants to know what that something is and the other half just wants to be there with her. I'm closing in behind Mickey, passing tree after tree, house after house. The path isn't always level. At the moment it's going down, but once we turn at the corner, it'll be level, and once we get close to the next corner, it'll go up. Instead of following the path, Mickey makes a sharp turn, and now we're riding on the grass, up the main mound, down the main mound, going in weird circles and big waves until Mickey comes to a full stop between two trees. I stop right next to him.

"Why did you stop?" I ask.

"I'm tired. And thirsty."

"Yeah."

"Do you want to come over later?" he asks. "I want to show you a new game I bought."

"Okay."

"It's called *Mouse Trap*. You'll really like it, Red, I swear! You have to come over."

"I'll have to ask my ma, though."

"Do you want to or not?"

"I do. I want to."

"Red?"

"Yeah?"

"Are you gonna ask your mom for a road racing set, like the one I have?"

"I don't know," I tell him, spinning the pedal with my shoe.

"We'd be able to play at your place and mine. Tell her it's for your birthday."

"Yeah. We'll see."

"You can just ask her."

I don't answer, but he knows I want one. He also knows that if Ma can't afford any twenty-dollar race car, she certainly can't afford a road racing set. I wish I had what Mickey has 'cause I'd never get bored, and he knows it. I told him so a while back.

"Yeah." I push my bike forward. "Say, let's go to the bridge."

"To see Lacey?"

"No."

"You like her, Red. I know."

"I don't… It's not what you think."

"Does she know you like her?"

"I never said I did, Mickey. We're just friends."

I start pedalling toward the bridge, with Mickey behind me. We lay our bikes on the grass below the bridge and walk up to Lacey and Cara and crouch beside them. There's a caterpillar between them, all furry. Cara's petting it with a stick, and Mickey says it's ugly. Lacey says it's not, and then Mickey says it is. I agree with Mickey but keep quiet.

"I want to keep it," Lacey says. "Watch it grow and turn into a butterfly. I think it's going to be purple."

"Why purple?" Mickey asks.

"I don't know. I have a feeling, that's all."

"Did you know caterpillars are herbivorous?" Cara asks us, still petting it with the stick.

"No," I say. What does she mean?

"And they're rich in protein," she adds. "And they're a source of silk."

Cara is nine and knows more, I guess. Sometimes I don't understand her at all. I ask her how she knows these things about caterpillars.

"My dad told me."

"What's sill?" I ask her.

"I don't know. It's *silk*. *S-I-L-Q-U-E*."

There's Finn, out on his balcony. He sees us and takes the stairs. I watch his body slowly disappear behind the fence then reappear as soon as he opens the backyard door. He's walking toward us, getting bigger and bigger. The sun is making his hair lighter, turning it into a gold-brown, and his eyes are dark, almost black. He stops beside us and looks down, his eyes now blue-green.

"That's one ugly caterpillar," he points out. "What are you going to do with it?"

"Nothing," Lacey says. "We just want to touch it."

"That's pretty stupid," he says.

"Lacey thinks it's going to be purple," Mickey says, and steps off the bridge to get his bike.

He starts pedalling when I tell him to wait up. I leave the bridge and hop on my bike, and now we're off. I'm leading the way, watching the tree leaves shake in the wind, smelling meat on the barbecue somewhere to my left, and then Lacey shouts, "No! Stop!" I ride back to the bridge. Lacey and Cara are walking away while Finn's heading back to his house like nothing happened. I let my bike fall on the grass and run up to them.

"What's wrong?" I ask Lacey. "What is it?"

"Just go," Cara says.

Lacey looks sad and angry. "Finn killed it. He killed it," she says.

They're walking to Cara's backyard.

"Why?" I ask.

Cara opens her backyard door. "Go away," she says, and closes the door in my face.

Mickey's waiting for me on the deck of the bridge. When I join him there, I find the caterpillar all crushed—graveyard dead. There's Finn, going up the steps to his balcony. I watch him with anger as he opens the balcony door, as he disappears like a ghost behind the curtains.

"Why did Finn have to do that?" I ask Mickey, staring at the dead caterpillar. "What was the point?"

"'Cause he's a villain. He destroys. That's what he does best."

"I don't get it, though. I don't get why people scare off cats or birds on the sidewalk or step on bugs. No wonder they're scared of us. It's not like they're doing anything bad, Mickey."

"Except spiders."

"Yeah."

"Spiders can do pretty bad things. And they're scary."

"It's sad when you think about what people do to creatures."

"Finn should know better, but he doesn't have a brain. He doesn't know right from wrong."

"I feel bad for him," I say, walking toward my bike. "That's someone I don't ever want to be."

HALF AN HOUR LATER I'm at the table, eating my supper. Ma's smoking next to me, and drinking. When Ma drinks, her voice changes. It gets louder and louder as if she thinks I can't hear her. She's shouting 'cause I can't finish my broccoli. It's hard to eat something you don't like, even if it's good for you. I've been trying to eat it all, but every time I take a bite something in me wants to push it out, like it's some kind of poison. I tell her I'm trying. I'm trying.

"Try harder! If I left so much as a fry, my mother would whack me on the head! Is that what you want, Redmond? You want me to whack you?"

"No, Ma."

My hands are flat on my lap, and they're not moving. They're afraid to move. Ma takes a sip of her drink. About half of her cigarette is gone. She's holding the other half between her fingers, with her elbow resting on the table. The TV is on. She's watching the news while I'm watching the smoke from her cigarette spiral and disappear near her face. I start poking a piece of broccoli with my fork to kill time, to make her believe I'm going to eat it. After a while Ma turns to me and gets angry. She starts shouting again, and then she leans in and whacks me on the head and says, "I told you to finish it! I told you, but you never listen. Just go to your room! Get out of my face!"

I go to the kitchen and empty my plate into the trash can. The kitchen counter is a mess. Plates and glasses and pots are lying about unclean. Ma's still shouting from the dining room. We can see each other 'cause there's no wall or door separating the rooms, and my eyes are burning. I don't want to cry in front of her, but I can't help it. I can't help it.

5

The sun is out. I'm sitting in the shade against a tree trunk, eating a chicken and lettuce sandwich. Candy's lying beside me on a beach towel, staring at the leaves or crops of the sky. We're having a picnic along our local bike path among cyclists and pedestrians, squirrels and other picnickers. It was Candy's idea to come out here so we could spend some quality time together. The fact that we haven't quarrelled at all this whole week is a big step in the right direction, though I'm still having trouble dusting off our last argument, which was pointless to say the least. Frankly I think she owes me an apology, but we both know that'll never happen. Sometimes I find myself reliving clips of the argument in my head, changing my replies on purpose to make them more damaging. I don't feel any better afterward. If anything, I feel even more frustrated, more angry at both of us. *A drunk with no friends*—that was her very last punch, the ultimate blow; even now it's nagging at me. Still hurting like a bruise not because it was rude but because it was true. Knowing truths about me doesn't give her or anyone else the right to use them as weapons. Not everything you know about a person should be said openly. Not everything, I think.

"My friend Elena…she's coming to town with her fiancé in a month or two—or maybe three, I'm not sure. But I want to invite them for supper."

"Elena?"

"From university. You don't mind, do you?" she asks, turning to look at me.

I shake my head but receive no smile, no touch in return. My hand reaches for her leg, but my conscience tells me, *No, don't touch her, don't caress her,* so I go back to watching the canal and the people walking along the bike path. There's something about this midday scene—maybe the water?—that reminds me of the city's Old Port. I close my eyes, picturing a large pedestrian square with cozy vintage restaurants. Fireworks in the summer sky and music festivals. Rows of boats moored to the quay. And the river…

"I was just thinking about how useful my major was," she says, and my eyes reopen. "It was really a toss-up between finance and poli sci. I'm glad I chose finance."

"Poli sci? What's that again?"

"Political science."

"Yeah."

"Are you considering it?"

"Considering what? School?"

"Last time you said you were too old. You're not, you know."

Honestly I haven't thought much about going back to school. We've talked about the matter several times already, and every time I've felt stupid and unimportant.

"I'm still unsure," I tell her. "I'm not ready yet, I guess."

She raises herself to a sitting position and wraps her arms around her legs and says, "It's not like you *love* working at that school. You can do better."

"But we've talked about this. You know I like working at the school. You want me to go back 'cause you think I'm nothing."

"I never said that. I'm just saying you can do better."

Of course, Candy, of course. You're ashamed. I know you. Ashamed of telling your friends that your boyfriend—who has no fancy title or degree like you do, who doesn't earn what you earn—picks up trash and mops floors for a living.

Maybe she's afraid her friends will talk behind her back about her or about us as a couple. I've always wondered if Candy truly wants what's best for me or if she just wants me to succeed for her own benefit. Given her high standards, she certainly didn't expect me to drop out of high school after my fourth year. She tried to talk me out of it, and my refusal to obey her put a dent in our relationship. The reason I quit was because of Ma. Because she died in May of that fourth year, and I didn't see any reason to go on studying. If we're all going to die anyway, what's the point? So I quit school. But now I wish I hadn't. I don't think I can go back, though. I'm just not the same person anymore. And I'm scared of quitting my job because I like it and I'm good at it, and I might not get another job that I like and that I'm good at. I doubt Ma would've cared much about my career choice. Besides, no one in her family ever finished high school. My pa? I can't say. I've never met him, and Ma hardly spoke of him. She once told me I reminded her of him. My pa's name is Stanley, after his grandpa. Stanley Quinn—now that's a pretty cool name.

"Can we bike to the Old Port?" I ask her, changing the subject. "Would that be okay?"

"If you want." She opens her knapsack. "I still have to eat, though."

"That's fine."

I'm about to close my eyes again when I hear her sigh and say, "Anyway, do what you want."

"What?"

"It's your life," she says, and starts eating.

IN THE WEE HOURS of the following morning I wake up from a troubling dream, and I'm afraid to go back to sleep. Most of the time I forget the details, but this dream was different. It was like an open wound, still unhealed, still hurting. It wasn't about my job or yesterday's picnic. Nor was it anything else I'd done recently. I was back in that hospital, in that dull white room where Ma was dying, and her face was blurry. It was only the two of us, and I couldn't touch her. No matter how hard I tried I couldn't hold her hand or embrace her. She kept repeating something in the hospital bed. I think it was, *Will you stay? Will you stay with me?* I didn't—or maybe I couldn't— answer. She looked very pale and bony, her hair thin and sickly. I remember saying, *Ma. It's me, Ma. I'm here. I won't go*, or something like that. *Don't go*, she kept saying in desperation. I couldn't understand why. Why would I go? *But I won't go, Ma. I'm here.* And I told her I was proud of her, I was glad to be hers. That's when she smiled, and her smile made me cry, and I told her she did good. I told her, *Don't leave me. You can't leave,*

Ma. If you do, I'll go with you. She smiled some more, but only briefly, faintly. Then my eyes opened, and she was gone.

6

There he is on a swing, eating Cole's sandwich while the trees in the darkness murmur. At this hour he's the only visitor in the park among slides and teeter-totters, black bushes and trees. He has his grocery cart behind him near the bench he'll be sleeping on, and below this bench are his shoes, caked with filth and worn out beyond repair. He's taking his time, enjoying every mouthful of the ham and the bread as though each bite were his last. But as much as he'd love to eat it all he needs to ration it wisely. He downs the carton of soy milk he saved up for this evening and wraps the half-eaten sandwich, which he puts back into his cart.

"Now where are you?" he says, searching for the thriller novel he bought at a garage sale for fifty cents.

Even without much light, the lamppost being too far away from the bench, he's eager to read a bit of it before going to sleep. His hands are digging, displacing junk—plastic cups, a sullied beach towel, two tennis balls, an empty cigarette pack—creating more chaos. Did I forget it somewhere? But wasn't it right here? he asks himself, thinking, still searching, the late-night crickets whistling perpetually in his ears. It doesn't take long before he finds something much more important, something soft hidden underneath a flattened Kleenex box: a small stuffed animal, a kind of rabbit-dog hybrid with beige fur and black buttony eyes.

"Max!" he exclaims. He presses the animal to his cheek, petting it as though it were alive. "Oh, it's so nice to see you again, my friend... I know... You're right, it's my fault. I'm sorry..."

Max, his friend and confidant, his travelling companion of many years, disappeared under a bridge one evening while the beggar, leaning into his cart, was at it again—shuffling his things around in search of a snack. All the tossing and the digging, fuelled by hunger, sent Max tumbling to a spot near the bottom, where it remained and was forgotten.

"I'm all right in case you're wondering. I'm fine," he says, and stares off into the distance. He can feel now, coursing through him like his own blood, night's energy, replenished and supreme, luring him into darker spaces. "I was about to go for a stroll... Yes, it's late... It is, but it's the perfect time. There's no one but us out here. Just you and me, Max. Two old pals," he says, having already forgotten about the novel.

With Max snuggled against his chest, the beggar sets off on a leisurely walk, leaving his shoes and his cart behind. He's on a mount, high above the downtown area, high above all the places he usually spends his time begging. He passes a tethered bicycle, stepping on overlapping shadows, looking across the street at the trees, at their upper leaves yellowed by lamplight.

A car passes by every now and then. Air conditioners hiss monotonously on first-storey floors. And over there, in the distance, he sees a figure in the dark diminishing, a small shadow moving among larger shadows.

There's no better time, he thinks. No better place than this, away from it all. If he could, if night could last for days and not hours, he'd stay out here under the stars, wandering the streets like a lone phantom in the darkness, in night's silence, while everyone else is sleeping.

"Where should we go?" he says, more to himself than to his stuffed animal. "I know you want to, but we can't. It's not the same anymore… Me?… Of course I won't. Why would I do such a thing?" he says, approaching the end of the block. "It's you and me out here. It's always been us… That won't ever happen. I'm not trading you for anyone, for anything, I won't do it. I'm not leaving… I won't ever leave you, Max, I promise."

Soon after crossing the next intersection, the beggar stops for a moment in the lamplight, along the edge of the sidewalk, to listen.

The wind is speaking to him through the trees. Speaking in tones that remind him of a past adventure, a conversation he once had with an old friend, and almost immediately he's seized with a sweet melancholy, a longing for moments of his youth that were once so meaningful to him, so joyful, and shared.

The beggar walks on a little longer, reminiscing, whispering to himself, before finally calling it a night. When he returns to the park, a wave of relief washes over him: All of his things are still there. He unfurls his sleeping bag on the bench and tucks himself in. Max is there with him, lying face up on his chest.

Up there, beyond the dead and the living, is his favourite summer sky: a calm blue-black sea, with stars twinkling, blotted by dark clouds, and the moon's crescent smile. Tonight's biggest cloud is shaped like an *L*, of all letters. The beggar follows the *L* closely, willingly, as it steers its way toward the moon.

"What should I do tomorrow...?" he says, feeling adventurous. "You say that 'cause *you* want to go there, not me." Though deep down, the beggar knows he wants to. Before sleep carries him off to another world, he says, barely more than a whisper, "No, it won't rain tomorrow. We'll have to wait. Let's wait and see... Should we?" He's almost certain. "I'm so glad I found you, Max. I'm glad... It won't rain, I'm sure. It'll be fine... Not tomorrow... Tomorrow..."

7

I'm with Ma, at the grocery store. Every Sunday before noon we go there, unless Ma's working for extra cash. If there's something I enjoy doing with Ma, it's grocery shopping (our only regular outing) 'cause I can usually get her to buy me something I like, so long as it's cheap. Last time Ma bought me a bag of ketchup chips, and the time before that a bag of marshmallows, which I ate in less than a day. So far I've passed each aisle twice, but I still can't decide whether I want something chocolatey or nothing at all. Ma wants to make some spaghetti and shepherd's pie this week, so she had me get the tomato and corn cans for her. I put them into the grocery cart on top of the dry spaghetti noodles and frozen salmon.

"What else, Ma?"

"Just a minute," she says, checking the dates on two milk cartons. "July twentieth… July fifteenth… Okay." She puts the worst of the two back on the shelf. "The butter, honey. Get me one stick."

"What about the potato sack?"

"It's too heavy, Redmond. Get the butter."

What she doesn't understand is that I'm strong and can carry it for her like a grown-up, but she never lets me. She should know I'm not like most kids. I do many grown-up things. I take care of her when she doesn't feel well, and I always look after myself when she goes out, while most kids can't take care of themselves or even their pet.

Up ahead are the yogurts and cheeses, along with a few grocery shoppers driving their loaded carts, some headed toward me, others away from me, curving here and there like baby cars on a two-lane street. I imagine myself turning into a car; I'm making my way past one cart, past a bunch of dairy products on one side and soda drinks on the other, past two more carts until I reach the butter and margarine section, where I park myself between a tall couple. I take the butter and set out to find Ma. Carts are passing me, but I'm not driving fast; I'm taking my time, looking at foods I've never seen or tried. Then I see *her*.

I press on the brakes next to a shelf of sauces. It's her, I know it is. She's chewing gum, blowing a pink bubble now, walking with her hand gripping the front of the cart her father's pushing, and there's her mother behind them, grabbing something from a shelf. She doesn't know I'm there 'cause she's not looking straight ahead but to the left. Instead of walking up to her I turn around and leave the aisle, feeling a little nervous. I find Ma and her cart two aisles later. I run up to her and put the butter into one corner of the cart.

"Anything else, Ma?"

"No, honey. Nothing else," she says, stopping to grab a bag of flour.

"Okay, I'll be back."

I don't wait for her to answer. I just go, eager to know what Lacey's doing. I find her alone, staring at chocolate bars right above her head. Slowly, quietly, I sneak up to her and stop at her side, expecting her to scream, to laugh at herself for having screamed. She turns to me, shocked but in a good way, her eyes glowing even, her lips forming a pretty smile.

"Red! What are you doing?"

"I thought you'd scream."

"Why would I scream?"

"I had a feeling you'd be scared. What are you looking at?"

"All these chocolate bars," Lacey says. "I don't know which one I want. Have you ever tried this?" She points her finger at a huge chocolate bar called Toblerone.

"Never tried."

"They're shaped like tiny mountains. They come in different sizes, but this is the biggest, I think."

I check the price. "It's too expensive. Ma won't buy it."

"What about this?" she asks, walking up to a stack of Oreo cookies farther into the aisle.

Now that's something I may want from Ma after all. I haven't eaten an Oreo in a very long time.

"Oreos, yeah. They're good. They're real good."

"I'm going to ask my parents if they can buy me a pack," she says, and takes a box with her.

I take one, too, so I can show it to Ma. I find her in the meat section.

"Ma! Ma, I know what I want."

I show her the box between my hands, and she says, "Oreo cookies? No."

"Why not?"

"You still have a box of oatmeal cookies to finish, remember?"

"But I want this. You said I could."

"I never said that. The answer is no."

"Lacey's getting a box."

"I said no, Redmond!" she snaps. "Just put it back."

I go back to the cookie section, annoyed and angry, and put the box where it was on the shelf. A short while later Lacey comes back empty-handed.

"They said yes."

I nod.

"You know what? My parents are talking to your mother."

"Oh, yeah?"

"Come," she says. "You can talk to my parents."

I don't want to go, but I walk with her anyway. Grown-ups don't interest me, and I never quite know what to say to them unless I'm talking to Ma. Maybe that's 'cause Ma understands me best; she's kind of like an older and wiser version of me, and there she is now, nodding at Lacey's father as we close in on them. Suddenly Lacey starts skipping, moving ahead of me, but I refuse to skip like a girl, so I just keep walking. When I get to Ma, I grab hold of the cart handle and set my eyes on Lacey's parents. Their clothes are nice and clean like Lacey's, and their faces alone tell me they're very school smart.

"So this is the man of the house," her father says.

"He is," Ma tells him, putting her hand on my shoulder.

I look down at the floor, my face heating up a little. I look back up and see Lacey smiling at me, her eyes glowing again, and I turn my head up even more toward Ma, who still has her hand on my shoulder, who's letting me know with her eyes that she's proud of me.

"He's a bit shy," she adds, rubbing my shoulder.

"You must be glad school's over," Lacey's father tells me.

"Very much."

"What grade will you be in?" Lacey's mother asks.

"Four."

"That's good! I was just telling your mother about next week's baseball game and that you're welcome to join us."

Knowing I'll be lectured if I say yes, I don't answer.

"That's very nice of you," Ma says, "but Redmond has certain things to do, don't you, Redmond?"

I nod, even though I shouldn't.

"That's too bad," Lacey's father says. "But maybe he'd like to come with us to the movies this afternoon. How about that?"

My eyes widen. The last time I went to the movie theatre was last year, and I would very much like to go. I look up at Ma for a yes, a smile, even a wink—any kind of yes.

"Oh, no," Ma says, letting go of my shoulder. "No, he can't today." She pushes the cart a little.

"We promise to bring him back before supper."

"No, no, Redmond's busy today."

"Lacey would love some company, wouldn't you, Lacey? I don't mind paying."

Lacey's mother grabs his arm. "She said no, George. Let it go."

Ma's forcing herself to smile. "It was nice seeing you. And you, too, Lacey."

Lacey's mother tells us more or less the same thing, and then we leave in opposite directions. A short while later I feel a hand tugging at my T-shirt. I turn to find Lacey right there, in front of me. We're so close I start to notice details I usually never see, like the beauty mark on her left cheek.

"Don't go too far," Ma says without slowing down. "Come to the front in five minutes."

We leave Ma and walk toward the potato sacks. There's a silence between us, and I can't find anything to break it. But she does.

"Dad said you're the man of the house. Is that true?"

"I guess so. But I'm not a man."

"Isn't that a lot of work?"

"It is, Lacey. I can even pick up the potato sack over there."

We get to the potato section. Bending forward, I grab a sack and start pulling it toward me, but it's heavy—it's too heavy to pick up and carry.

"I thought I'd be able to. It's heavier than it looks."

"Do you think it weighs a ton?"

"Probably more."

"Anyway, you don't need to be big and strong to be in charge. Oh, I almost forgot!"

"What?"

"I want to show you something," she says, walking now.

I follow her, leaving the potato sack where it is. I watch her reach into her pocket for a piece of folded paper, which she begins to unfold.

"I drew it in the car," she says. "I wanted to give it to you later today, like in the evening."

She hands me the drawing. Two big happy faces are on the page, one with long, curly brown hair and the other without, and all around us—I mean all around the faces—are tiny yellow stars.

"It's for you," she says. "Keep it."

"Is that me?"

"You have to go, Red. Your mom's waiting."

"Yeah. We'll meet up later in the park, okay?"

"Okay." She turns her back to me and skips away, her pony-tail swinging.

I stare at the paper for a while before folding it up and putting it into my pocket. I start walking, thinking about what we might do later today, about stars, about me and Lacey under the stars.

MA'S AT THE COUNTER, packing our food into plastic bags. I run up to her and start packing what's left. Within seconds I notice something in one of the bags: a box of Oreo cookies.

"But Ma?" My eyes are real big, and my mouth can't seem to close.

"It's all right," she says, then looks up for a moment (maybe at Lacey's parents approaching?—I can't be sure). "I'm happy if you're happy."

"I am. Thank you, Ma." I wrap my arms around her.

"All right," she says, rubbing my back. "All right, honey. Let's go home."

8

The inevitable happened, so now we're not talking. She's in our bedroom, blowing her nose every five seconds like someone battling the flu. I have no desire to go in, let alone comfort her. I'm in the living room, sipping a beer on the couch, waiting for one of us to do something, say something—*what* exactly I can only guess. One thing is clear: Our relationship has to change; otherwise we're wasting our time. There's no use being with a partner who wants you to become someone you don't want to be. We're exact opposites, that's what we are. Opposites who have feelings for each other but can't find middle ground. I think it's time—maybe it's time we call it quits. Maybe what I truly need is a fresh start, without her.

Earlier this week we had an argument at the dinner table. I told Candy I wasn't in the mood to see Molly and Tom, her former colleagues. They're both real nice people, but whenever they come over I feel left out. Work is always their main topic of conversation, so the three of them communicate in a language I barely understand. They also talk about people I don't know, people I've never met before, and more often than not I tune out after a while. But despite everything, I have nothing against them coming over. I just don't want to be there when they do. Anyway, they're her friends, not mine.

So this evening, when Molly and Tom were at our doorstep, I wasn't there with her to greet them. I was at a twenty-four-hour diner, which is a ten-minute walk from my school. After that I went to a bar and stayed there until eleven, more or less. When I arrived home half an hour ago, the guests had already left and Candy was sitting on the couch, waiting for me, looking upset. I gave her my reasons, but she rejected them all. She told me how antisocial, how disrespectful, how distant I was in her eyes, and went on to say that I excel at nothing. *Nothing.* Hearing that last word was the final straw for me, and I fired back. I told her she was irritating, condescending, overly demanding. I meant every word I said, and my voice had knives in it just like hers. But seeing her cry in front of me almost brought me to tears. I couldn't say anything more at that point, and neither could she. Now the air around me is filled with an oppressive tension. I wish I could turn back the clock and change everything, but it's too late. What's done is done.

I can't hear her now. She must've stopped crying or cried herself to sleep. With teary eyes I get up and walk out the door. I make my way down the corridor, down flights of steps until I'm out of the apartment building, out among parked cars and trembling leaves, shadows and lamplight. I feel better already. I can breathe better, too. The bike path along the canal is only a few blocks away. I go there and sit on the first bench I see. There's a couple cuddled together on a nearby bench, but they don't notice me. I reach into my left pocket for a cigarette and into my right for the lighter.

Candy might be wondering where I am at the moment. Usually I write her a note when I leave the apartment for a late-night walk, but this time the thought slipped my mind. Given tonight's quarrel, I doubt she even cares. Sometimes I wish I could lend her my mind so she could understand me completely. Maybe that way she'd learn to accept our differences, embrace my faults even, my weaknesses.

Taking a drag, I turn my attention back to the couple. They're kissing. Looking like a picture of true love in this chilly darkness. She smiles at him. Laughs at something he just whispered in her ear, and then kisses him. If only we were like them, I tell myself, turning away. If only our bond were that strong.

It's one o'clock when I finally head home. I take my time, thinking some more, gazing every now and then at the stars, dim white dots fading in and out like neon signs. I hope she's sleeping because I wouldn't know what to say to her. The closer I get to the apartment, the more nervous, the more uncertain I feel about going back in.

Minutes later I find myself facing the apartment door. I try not to make a sound as I push it open and remove my shoes. The lights are out, the door to our room less than halfway open. I tiptoe into our room, where I see her lying on her side, lying so still I can't tell whether she's awake or asleep. I take my clothes off and get into bed. My eyes are wide open as I lie there on my back, thinking, waiting.

"Where were you?" she asks, not moving.

"Out. At the canal."

After a brief silence she says, "Do you love me?"

Frowning, I turn my head toward her. "Of course I do. Why would you ask me that?"

"Never mind."

A second silence creeps into the room. I can hear myself swallowing, my own shallow breathing.

"I wanted to take some air, to think a bit."

She turns over on her back. My gut tells me she's expecting an apology, or waiting for me to say, *You were right*, or, *I was wrong*.

"I'm sorry I hurt you."

Instead of answering me she turns over on her side again, her back facing me. Tears are welling up quickly, falling on my pillow. They keep falling and falling, and now I'm sniffling and I don't think I'll be able to sleep.

The silence is too loud.

9

He awakens without Max, his stuffed animal. The sun isn't up yet. From the bench he sees no one, hears nothing save the occasional bird chirping. Once out of the sleeping bag, the beggar puts his shoes back on; picks up Max, who was lying on the ground an arm's length away; and goes to his cart where his breakfast awaits him.

What will I eat today? he asks himself. What can I eat? With Max back in his cart, the beggar brings to the bench a granola bar and some bottled tap water, thinking about where to go next. Like always, he hopes to get a decent amount of change by the end of the day, and if all goes well, he may treat himself to a doughnut (either a honey cruller or a jelly dough-nut)—just the thought of it makes his mouth water. "No," he says aloud. No, he doesn't want to wait. He'll buy himself a doughnut this very morning.

Minutes after eating his breakfast, he caps the empty bot-tle and puts it back into his cart along with the sleeping bag, leaving only the granola bar wrapper on the bench. He sets off in the predawn light, the cart wheels screeching non-stop on the sidewalk. The noise will wake everyone up, he thinks, yet he walks on anyway, determined as he is to get down the mount and buy himself a doughnut.

At some point the beggar takes a left, then walks straight ahead until he reaches an intersection. The funicular is in full view of him across the street. When he gets there, he stops for a moment to survey the landscape before him. From up here he can see it all, the whole of the city in all its splendour: skyscrapers dull grey and matted silver, soaring into the sky; smaller buildings all scattered—gargantuan cylinders glowing here and there with squares of pale yellow, cubes with brown pyramidal tops, rectangular prisms set upright; two bridges spanning the same river; so many rooftops, so many black windows and coloured lights; knots of bushlike trees; birds.

The funicular takes him and his cart down the slope, all the way down to level ground. The café he's heading to is open 24-7, and he's almost there. He just needs to turn left at the next intersection, walk past a couple of stores, then make a right. But luck isn't in the cards this morning: As he passes a sports store, someone intercepts him. Someone he isn't too fond of, sitting on the sidewalk next to a lamppost.

"Joey," the beggar says, eyeing the beer bottle his acquaintance is holding. Empty ones are spread out around the man, and on the ground near his knees is a flat-brimmed cap, dirt-stained and without coins.

"You! Cart man!" Joey cries, lifting his free hand in mid-air. "You! Why? Why did you?"

The beggar doesn't understand his question, nor does he want to.

The moment the beggar pushes his cart, Joey yells at him: "Hey, cart man! Stop!" Joey puts his beer on the ground and struggles to his feet.

"You!" he goes on, wobbling this way and that, his finger pointed at the beggar. "You never said hi! I saw you!"

"No, Joey. You didn't see me anywhere."

"Yes, I did! Don't lie to me, I know you! You hate me, say it. Everyone hates me."

At that moment Joey grabs hold of the beggar's cart.

"Get your hands off," the beggar warns, glancing around him.

"Shut up! You knew I was there! You knew but you didn't say anything. Who the fuck do you think you are?" he yells, shaking the cart vigorously, furiously, his eyes reddening.

"Get your hands off my cart!" the beggar shouts. "Get your hands off, I said!"

"No, you get off! You're like *them*, like the cops! You hear?"

Joey frees the cart, goes up to the beggar's face, and seizes his arm.

"Don't touch me," the beggar says, his voice and face solemn. "Joey, I'm warning you now, don't touch me."

"You're like the cops!" Joey yells again. "You're all the same! You all treat me like a dog!"

"I said don't touch me!"

The beggar pushes Joey away. Reaching into his pocket, he pulls out a handful of coins and tosses them on the ground, sending them rolling and wobbling in every direction. Joey, still yelling, gets down on his knees to pick up the change while the beggar, frightened and shaken, thrusts his cart forward without looking over his shoulder. He rushes past a bookstore, past a sushi bar, then turns left at the corner but keeps going, feeling pursued. At the next corner he finally stops and turns around. His eyes soften; his heartbeat slows down. No one's there.

The beggar walks on slowly, catching his breath as he goes. When he reaches Beignes & Coffee less than a minute later, he takes out what's left in his pockets and calculates the total. He doesn't have enough.

"Damn you, Joey," he says. "Always drinking. Ruining everything."

But am I really any different? he thinks, putting his coins away. Don't I drink, too, like so many of the homeless? Like the lonely? The depressed? He pulls out his wallet and looks down at his four twenties, his two tens, his five. He knows it's possible; he knows he could always use his five, but should he make an exception?

With a heavy sigh, the beggar closes his wallet and walks on in disappointment, searching for a convenient spot to panhandle. He parks his grocery cart next to a tree and settles himself on the ground, under the leaves, trying to clear his mind of Joey and their altercation, his doughnut craving, all the coins he threw away, and to replace them with thoughts of today's plans and projected earnings.

It won't take long, he tells himself, listening, waiting. Soon the early risers will be coming out like the sun. They'll be pouring out of subway stations and city buses and throng the streets, making their usual collective noise. Most will ignore him; most won't even look his way, but he doesn't blame them. If he were in their shoes, he'd do just the same.

10

Candy always had a big crush on me. She said so when we first started dating. I still remember our first date like it was yesterday. It was at a restaurant, on her sixteenth birthday. She'd gotten all kinds of presents from her family, her school friends. From me she got only two, but they were two things I knew she'd like: a bracelet with little heart beads all over it and a jumbo bag of her favourite cinnamon jujubes.

Later that evening we went to some random club downtown. Although we weren't adults we took a chance, and the bouncer let us in without asking for ID. We were on the dance floor for a long time, under these blue rotating lights that made everyone look kind of sci-fi, mysterious and all. At some point the music brought us so close together we kissed. The kiss just happened—like magic, without warning—but it was real. It was a kiss that meant something to me, that felt right. We were only teens at the time, discovering ourselves and each other.

We were still at the same stage in our lives where inexperience was—and still is—the norm. Maybe that's why we got along better then. Our lives were more compatible.

Candy. She's been out of town since yesterday for some business conference, and she'll be back tomorrow evening. While she's probably out exploring or having a fancy meal, I'm heading on foot to Stanley, a bar near the downtown area. Stanley isn't popular, but it's quiet, and quiet is what I like. Candy says I go there too often, and she's afraid I'll become like her stepfather, who's an alcoholic, or like my ma. I think she's just overreacting.

When I enter the bar I find, as expected, only a few customers. I take a seat on a stool in a corner. No one's looking my way except the bartender.

"So what will it be this time?" he asks.

"Scotch."

As he pours the drink into a square glass, I can't help but notice the dragon tattoo on his forearm, the dim sheen of his scalp under the ceiling lights. I take a sip of the Scotch and stare at the liquor bottles all lined up against the wall, the marble bar counter, my hands. Minutes later a young woman comes in and sits four stools away from me, placing her pink purse on the bar counter. She orders a bourbon and catches me observing her but doesn't look away. She's beautiful, I can't lie. Her hair has streaks of red in it, which I find pretty cool, and her skin looks as smooth as porcelain.

"Nice tattoo," she says, out of the blue, reaching for her glass. "Really nice."

What she's referring to (my first of three tattoos so far) is engraved on my left forearm: a cursive capital R in red and black, with green leaves along its tail and an orange-yellow sun shining above and behind it.

"*R* for Redmond, my name," I tell her. "Or just Red. Everyone calls me Red."

She smiles and takes a sip of her bourbon.

"I like the hair. Very original."

"Really?" she says.

"Yeah."

"I wanted something bold, you know? That catches the eye."

"It certainly does."

She laughs and takes another sip and says, "You wanna know what I see, Red?"

I'm not quite sure what she means. "Okay?"

"I see a quiet guy having, let me guess…a Scotch?" I nod, and she says, "He's having a Scotch, then, to decompress. And he has this…this charm about him—that's it. It's the eyes." She lifts her glass to her lips. "Or that nervous smile. Am I hot or cold?"

"Pretty hot." I watch her take another sip.

"And so this guy—who's blushing at the moment—well, he's just bored out of his mind. But then he sees this lady walk up to the bar, this lady with the coolest head—I mean the coolest hair—and now he wants to know…" She leaves her sentence hanging for a moment. "And that's about it!" she says, laughing at herself.

"That's…that's really good." I scratch my head, smiling at the bar counter.

She gets up, grabs her purse, and sits on the stool right next to me. I nod toward the drink she left behind, so she gets up again, laughing.

"That's just me. Typical me," she says, returning with her drink in hand.

I ask her if she comes to Stanley often, because I've never seen her here before.

She shakes her head and says, "No, it's only my second time," and tells me a bit of her life story.

Like me she was born and raised here, in the city of Willobrooks. She didn't stay, though. After high school she left for California to attend university, where she studied in business. Now she lives in New York City, close to Central Park, and has a roommate who's an architect. Not long ago she landed a new job as a business development manager, but she's only starting it in a few months. Until then she's back in Willobrooks, visiting her parents and staying with a friend. She says her family travelled a lot when she was younger. They went to places like Egypt and Japan, France and Germany and Australia—places I can't imagine myself going to. I haven't met anyone (not even Candy) who's done as much as she has, young or old.

"What about you?" she asks. "What's your story?"

I've never shared my life story, not with anyone. It's certainly nothing compared to hers. I know she won't like it, and besides, "There's nothing much to say. It's all boring."

"I'm sure it's not. Tell me."

"Well, I don't really know where to start."

"What do you do?"

"I'm… I work at a school. It's not far away from my apartment, so I just have to walk there." After a short pause I say, "And I've never been out of the country."

"Ever?"

I shake my head.

"Never taken the airplane?"

"Nope—not yet anyway. But I'm happy here. It's what I know best, I guess. My ma and me—we were always poor, so travelling wasn't in the cards for us. She had to pay for every-thing 'cause my pa wasn't there. He was never there, not even when I was born, so that's that."

"Must've been hard, though, just the two of you."

"For my ma. He made everything worse, by leaving her. I'll never forgive him for that. I used to think about him a lot. I used to think he'd come one day. Now I couldn't care less if he's alive or dead."

"I see…" she says, and looks at her glass. "So what do you do at your school?"

"Well…" I clear my throat. "I'm part of the school person-nel. There's a name for it…the maintenance staff."

"Like a janitor?"

I nod. "Like that."

I finish my Scotch and order another one. She orders a Scotch, too, and while the bartender's refilling our glasses, she asks me if I'm taken. The truth is that I want to lie. I don't want to disappoint her because part of me wants her. And because another part of me wants her to want me.

"I've been with my girlfriend, Candy, for about ten years. We've known each other since childhood."

"Candy? That's an unusual name."

"I call her Candy 'cause she loves eating all sorts of candy, especially jujubes. But her real name is Cara."

"Cara?" she says. "Cara."

"What about your name?"

Her eyes are steady. "Stella. My name's Stella."

"Well, Stella," I reply, taking a sip of my Scotch, "Candy and me—we're…" I bring my hand up and rock it a bit. "Ten years of dating is a long time, but we've only been living together for the past two years or so. Before that, life was better all around; we were happier. And then we moved in together. It was great for a while, but things started to change. They just did."

"I know what you mean," she says. "It's happened to me, too."

Instead of asking me more questions she starts talking about some of her past relationships—about that time when she threw her ex's clothes out the window in a fit of rage, when another ex locked her out of her own apartment, and when she had sex out in the open. "Twice," she points out, "twice I had sex with him in the ocean!"

For a moment I stop listening. All I can think about is us having sex in the ocean. I'd love to invite her over, but what if she refuses? When she finishes her sentence, I say, "You know, I was wondering... Would you like to come over, maybe have a drink?"

"Another drink? At your place?"

I nod. "If you're free, of course. Unless you're busy."

"I don't know. I mean, your girlfriend—"

"She's not in town. Candy and me... It's complicated."

"I can see that," she says, and finishes her drink.

"So?" I ask. "Is that a yes?"

STELLA DROVE ME HOME in a red Acura she doesn't actually own; her parents are letting her drive one of their cars while she's here.

I turn on the light.

"This is it," I say. But I'm embarrassed now, with her by my side. Only now do I realize how untidy my apartment is.

While she looks around, I prepare her a drink like I said I would. She enters my room. I follow her with two glasses, one in each hand, and apologize for the mess. Candy's papers are lying on the floor, along with some of her clothes and some of my own. The bed is unmade, drawers are open with shirts and underwear sticking out of them, and there's my nightstand, looking like a small dining room table with my coffee mug and a plate of unfinished apple pie still sitting on it.

Stella laughs. "You clearly haven't seen my room."

She takes both glasses and puts them on top of Candy's drawer chest. She walks up to me in the semi-darkness. For a moment we just stare at each other; it's as if we're waiting for one of us to make the first move. My hand reaches for her right cheek, then the back of her neck. I lean forward, pull her toward me, and kiss her. Our bodies fuse. I feel a hand warming my neck, another hand travelling down to my cock and stroking it, hardening it now. After the kiss she backs up toward the bed, bringing me with her while I unbutton my pants, while I look deep into the dark wells of her eyes, so mesmerizing up close, so mysterious.

WE'RE IN BED, NAKED. I'm lying on my side, facing her, my hand touching her thigh. Stella's sitting up with the pillow cushioning her back, and she takes a puff at her cigarette. I watch her eyes move, wondering what she's looking at. Candy's clothes? All of those lipsticks and necklaces on her drawer chest? My gaze shifts from the length of her neck to her apple-sized breasts, to the fleshy part of her leg, her straight little toes. I feel a slight stirring now, in my loins.

"I hope she doesn't mind," she says.

"I don't. I don't regret it, any of it."

"What's she like?" she asks, turning to me. "Or what does she look like? Your girlfriend."

"She's tall."

She laughs—why, I can't say. "Okay. Is she taller than you?"

"We're about the same—five foot six, maybe seven. But for a woman I find her pretty tall. She's a blonde. Straight hair all the way down to her upper back. She styles it a lot. Maybe it's a girl thing? I think it is, like all the shoe-shopping girls do, or shopping in general."

"They're all girl things."

"And her eyes are a gorgeous, sapphire blue. It's a rare eye colour."

She asks me for a picture of her. Obeying her like a pupil, I walk out of the room and come back with a framed picture from the living room that was under a stack of newspapers. The picture was taken a while back at a restaurant. There's Candy, all radiant and happy in my arms. Although she's just an image between my hands, I feel like she's really here, a miniature version of her watching me, looking so innocent, and now I can't help but feel horrible, ashamed—guilty. I hand Stella the picture. She makes a small O with her mouth to let the smoke out and brings the picture closer to her eyes.

"She's very pretty," she says.

"She is."

"Beautiful like all my friends. I think I'm the least beautiful among them. I've always felt that way about myself. Less pretty. Less everything, really."

"You're not less to me."

"You think so?"

I nod, and she says, "There was this one friend—one of my best friends at the time—she just had it all. She was everything I wanted to be. Smart and beautiful, responsible. Anyway, I used to pretend I was her. Sometimes I'd get so jealous I'd cry and say mean things about her to myself. I used to do that a lot, of course not so much anymore." She smiles, but fleetingly. "And I'd tell myself, *I'll never get a boyfriend. As long as she's there, I don't stand a chance.* There was someone, though. He… I had a huge crush on him. I didn't think he'd ever want someone like me—less pretty, less smart, always less—so I never did anything about it. He never got to be my boyfriend."

"His loss."

She lays the picture down between us on the bed and puffs out another O of smoke. "It was my loss, too."

11

Today marks a brand new chapter for us as a couple. We've waited so many years to live together, and now we finally have our own apartment.

"I can't wait to hang my London painting," Candy says, opening a cardboard box. "It'll look so great in our living room! I'm so excited! Aren't you?"

I walk up to her with the bed lamp in my hand and kiss the dimple on her cheek. "Of course I am."

"It's ours, Red. Our home."

Seems more like a ransacked warehouse than a real home, I tell myself as I stare at the unopened boxes stacked up against the living room wall, the coffee table cluttered with clothes and trinkets, the dining room in disarray. Even though all the furniture is here (two of Candy's school friends gave me a hand with the heavy loads earlier today), there's still a lot of unpacking to do.

Candy couldn't wait to move out of her parents' home. Not that her parents were strict or hard to live with, but she wanted more freedom, more time for us to be together. Of course, I agreed with her completely. My former apartment was too small and not to her liking, the neighbourhood uninviting, so we found something bigger (but affordable) near my school. Candy got her master's degree not long ago, and she'll start her first career job as a financial analyst next week. Her parents bought her a car as a graduation present, so travelling to and from work won't be a problem. I think it's safe to say our apartment was a very wise choice.

While Candy's busy taking out glasses and plates, I head over to the stack of unopened boxes and pick one up randomly. I bring it to the dining room table where her beauty creams are lying about and open the cardboard flaps.

"It's your school stuff," I tell her. "What do you want me to do?"

"You can put it on the bed. I'll take care of it later."

I carry the box to our room and take out the books one by one, reading the titles before laying them on the bed. The one in my hand has a brown cover with no lettering on it. I open the book to the very first page, where I see the word DIARY *in purple capitals.*

"You keep a diary?"

"What?"

"You have a diary here," I shout.

"Oh, yeah."

When she gets to the doorway, she looks at the book and says, "Yeah, that's my diary," and walks up to me with her hand outstretched.

"I didn't read anything."

She takes it from me and quickly checks the books still in the box and those already on the bed. "I know you didn't."

"I had no idea. You never mentioned anything about keeping a diary. Must be a recent thing?"

"Actually, no. I'm pretty sure I told you, though."

"Really?"

"A long time ago," she says, backing away. "You want a doughnut?"

"Yeah. Okay."

I follow her out of the room and into the kitchen, where the microwave and toaster are still unplugged, still waiting for their designated spot on the counter.

"How are your parents doing?" I ask her.

Before answering she gives me a chocolate-glazed doughnut. "My mom cried this morning, but my dad's taking it pretty well. It's going to be weird living without them. I've never lived with anyone else."

"You'll miss them, I know."

"Yeah. Them just being there, but it'll pass. I have you now," she says, reaching her hand out to hold mine. "You're the one I want."

I'm so proud of her, of what she's accomplished so far. To be honest, I would've gone nuts had I stayed in school for that long. But at the same time I'm glad school's over for her. Now she can focus her time and energy on her career, on making money. Candy doesn't seem to know I'm watching her. She's thinking, I'm sure, about what she plans on doing soon: hosting parties here, brunches with friends, cocktails and other social activities she couldn't organize under her parents' roof. When I think of our new home, I think of dinner dates on our balcony, movie nights in the living room, conversations about nothing and everything. More sex.

"Aren't you going to eat something?"

"Yeah, yeah," she says before opening the fridge. "Oh. Before I forget," she goes on, her hand disappearing for a moment, only to reappear with a strawberry yogurt, "maybe we can paint the walls green."

"Green?"

"Moss green. Something serene?" She opens a drawer next to the fridge, expecting to take a spoon, but finds no cutlery.

"You don't like white?" is all I manage to say instead of no.

"We'll see, I guess. Anyway, all this is temporary."

I stop chewing. "How so?"

"Well, it's only a matter of time before we move out and buy ourselves a house."

I'm not sure she realizes how much money we'd need for a down payment. I shrug, feeling a laugh coming up in my throat. "The spoons are in the box with the orange lid."

"That's fine," she says, reopening the fridge. "I'll eat it later."

She returns to the living room to unpack. I finish up the doughnut, watching her delicate hands move, her sunburnt shoulders, her pale legs. To celebrate today's occasion I should take her out tonight, somewhere nice and quiet under the stars, then bring her to an ice cream shop where she can have the sorbet of her choice. She would like that, I know. I'll surprise her, then, toward evening.

"Such a pretty couple," she says, holding a framed picture of us back in our late teens.

I go up to her and take it from her hand, bringing it close to my face. I was so thin, so small in that red-striped T-shirt with my hair uncombed and greasy. But I was happy, I really was. I still am, I guess. Just older and heavier now. Maybe even wiser, I hope.

"You were so cute," she says.

I lay the picture on the dining room table and go back to the living room, where I open a new box. For a while we don't say anything. All I hear between us is the sound of objects being unpacked *or put away. Some of the boxes I open are crammed full of Candy's clothes (which I pile on the bed) or her jewelry (which I leave on her dresser), while others contain all kinds of pantry essentials.*

As I enter the kitchen with a box of cutlery, Candy's wild getaway plan reaches my ears: "My friend's going on an all-inclusive trip with her boyfriend. Wouldn't that be great for us? I was thinking along the lines of Fiji. Or the Bahamas."

"That would be a pretty big trip," I tell her, wondering how much I'd have to spend for it.

"I know. But it would be a change of scenery. A place to relax without the daily routine."

"Well, I think you should—we should wait a bit. See how things go over the next few months?"

"Months?"

"You've lived with your parents your whole life, Candy. You said it yourself."

"What's that's supposed to mean?" she asks, turning to me with an album in her hands.

"I mean this is the first time you're going to be paying for all sorts of things. Your parents paid for your tuition, for your living expenses, but not anymore. You've got yourself a really good job, which you've earned, and that's awesome, but money goes away real fast. It just does. You don't know yet 'cause you haven't started. But I know."

"Oh, you do, don't you?" Candy says in a rather playful tone. She sets the album down on the coffee table and walks up to me, smiling.

"Wait until you pay part of the rent, the electricity bill, the food, the gas."

"You do realize I studied in finance." She puts her hand on my shoulder, smiling even more, not taking any of my remarks seriously.

"I do, Candy."

"Master's."

"Yeah. But it's just…knowing how much you spend on clothing, on all your cosmetics"—she kisses my cheek—"I doubt you'll save enough to buy a plane ticket this year"—she kisses the tip of my nose, then pinches it—"You get what I mean?"

"Hmm…" she says, still smiling but less, and walks back to the living room.

I'm about to put away the cutlery when she adds, "It's going to be great, you know."

"What is?"

"This new life of ours, right here," she says, opening a box. "My gut's telling me everything will be fine. We'll be just fine, Red. You'll see."

12

This time, Rex's it. We had a rock-paper-scissors match of three rounds. The last round was rock for me and scissors for him. He wasn't happy about losing to me, but I won fair and square. I'm just glad I can hide like the others. And who knows? Maybe I'll kick the ball and piss off Rex even more.

While Rex was counting up to thirty, Lacey and me ran off to the alleyway near the bridge. Cara followed us there, and now all three of us are crouching close together in the bushes. Rex's shouting a name, and I can tell from the loudness of his voice that he's far, too far for me to start worrying. Cara's giving Lacey one of those looks people give when they can't share something private with a friend 'cause someone else is present, and I'm that someone else.

"I wonder where Mickey is," I say, after a short while.

"No one cares about him but you," Cara says.

"He's my friend, Cara. I'll always care about him."

"Well, you have poor taste in friends."

Cara doesn't really like Mickey 'cause he didn't invite her to his birthday party this year. He invited Lacey, though, at my request. And so when Cara found out that Lacey had gone to his birthday party, she called him names and he told her to go to hell. Since then they've been ignoring each other a lot. Sometimes Mickey brings out popsicles for us, but he doesn't give any to Cara anymore. That just makes her hate him even more.

"Lacey wants to know if you like anyone."

"No, I don't, Cara," Lacey insists.

"She's shy."

"Cara, stop. It's not true."

"Shhh! Not so loud, Lacey," Cara says.

"Red, don't listen to her."

"Do you?" Cara asks me. "Do you like anyone?"

"No."

"Would you go out with Lacey? Or me?"

Her question makes me uneasy. I look down at the ground and say, "Why do you want to know?"

"It's just a question," Cara says.

The answer to her question is yes and no. Yes, I'd go out with Lacey, and, no, I wouldn't go out with Cara.

"What about you?" I ask. "Would you go out with me?"

"She would," Lacey says.

"Shut up, Lacey. Don't listen to her," Cara says. "Anyway, I asked you first."

I have a feeling she wants me to say, *Yes, I'd go out with you, Cara*, but I keep my yes and no answers to myself.

Before any of us can say anything else, we hear footsteps approaching. Every part of me (except my eyes) freezes for a moment. My heart's racing as the footsteps get louder. Cara's covering her mouth. Lacey's eyes are looking somewhere up, not blinking, not moving. Between the leaves I see the figure walking past us: an old man with glasses and white hair, who doesn't seem to know we're hiding in the bushes.

"It's okay. It's not Rex," I whisper to them, relieved.

Rex shouts Alf's name. Tired of crouching, the three of us kneel on the ground. Cara reaches into her pocket and takes out some folded paper, which she then unfolds to create an origami fortune teller. She asks me to pick either green, orange, red, or yellow. I pick red 'cause that's my name. She opens the origami for the *R*, then closes and reopens it for the *E* and finally the *D*. Now I have to choose a number among those I see, so I choose eight, my age. The origami's back in action, closing and opening while she's counting out loud from one to eight. Once again she asks me to choose a number, so I choose five. She flips open the flap of paper with the number five on it and reads my fortune out loud to me.

"You have a crush on me."

"What? No."

"Well, that's what it says," Cara answers. She shows me the handwritten message in green.

"It's not true," I say, looking at her, then at Lacey. "It's not true."

"*Fine*," Cara says, and puts the origami back into her pocket. Now we're all silent, doing nothing but waiting.

"Red! Red, come out!" Rex shouts.

The girls are as surprised as I am.

"But he didn't even come here," Lacey says.

I agree with her. "He's wrong, Lacey, that's what."

"Red! You're behind the bridge!"

"What are you going to do?" Cara asks me.

"Nothing. I'm staying here."

"Red, come out! You're behind the bridge! I saw your head, now come the fuck out!"

"He has no idea what he's saying. It's not even me."

"You have to tell him," Cara says. "You have to go."

I step out of the bushes, but I don't see Rex in the distance. He's probably somewhere close to the soccer ball. House walls and backyard fences make up the walls of each alleyway, acting as shields in a way. So as I walk toward the end of the alleyway, I stay close to the backyard fence to my left. When I get to the corner of the fence, I crouch and scan the park. There's Rex near the soccer ball on the main mound, along with two captives. He's not even looking in my direction; he's looking straight at the bridge! What an asshole.

"You're wrong, Rex!" I shout back, walking out of the alleyway and into the open. "I wasn't behind the bridge!"

"I saw you! I swear I did."

"Don't lie." I walk toward him. "How could that be if I was in the alleyway?"

"Because you switched hideouts, that's why! You went from there to there while I was running to call you out."

"That's not true."

"You're a cheater! A cheater!"

I run over to the bridge and see Aaron behind it.

"You thought it was me, but it was Aaron!" I shout from the bridge. "It was Aaron!"

"No, it was you! It was you! And now *you* have to be it. You broke the rules, so you have to be it!"

Hank and Finn come out from their hiding spot.

"Who thinks Red broke the rules?" Finn says. His question has us all looking at each other.

Hank and Finn raise their hands 'cause they hate me and want me to lose. Rex does the same 'cause he's a liar and an idiot. The captives raise their hands, too, but they're afraid; they just want to protect themselves.

"I don't care if your hands are raised," I say, while more people come out from their hiding spots to join the others on the main mound. "I didn't cheat. I was in that alleyway the whole time!"

"Everyone here thinks you did, so…"

"Just shut up, Rex!"

"You're a cheater!" he says. "A piece of shit!"

I push him, and then he pushes me, so I push him back I push him so hard he falls to the ground and now I jump on him and we exchange hits until a neighbour yells at us from his balcony and we stop. I get up and adjust my T-shirt, brushing off the grass and dirt on it, then walk out of the park with my head down, breathing hard, feeling all kinds of bad. Mickey shouts my name, but I keep walking.

"Red!" he shouts again, louder this time.

He catches up to me and puts his hand on my shoulder.

"Red, you okay?"

I avoid his eyes. "Yeah, I'm fine."

"I told Rex he's an idiot. You don't need to go, though. We can do something else."

"No, I want to go home."

"You sure? I can come with you."

"It's okay, Mickey. I'll see you tomorrow."

"Okay."

"Can you tell Lacey I'm going home?"

"I was going to tell her anyway."

"And that I'll see her tomorrow?"

"I was going to tell her that, too," he says. "I know, Red. I'll tell her."

I GO BACK HOME, thinking about the fight even though I don't want to. Ma's sitting in the living room with an album on her lap. The lights are not on. The see-through curtains are half closed, stirring a little, and the only sound I hear are my neighbour's footsteps above our floor. I make my way to the living room and sit on the couch next to Ma. She wraps her arm around me and takes a puff at her cigarette. I put my head on her shoulder and stare at the pictures before me: pictures of her when she was younger and of old people I don't recognize.

"Did you have fun?"

I shake my head, keeping my eyes down.

"Did they hurt you, honey?"

"No," I lie. "Who's that?" I put my finger on the black-and-white face of an old man sitting on his porch.

"My granddad. And right beside him is Dad—my daddy."

"They look happy, with their beers and all."

"Happy drunks," she says. "Spent their time drinking, not being fathers. And now look what I've become. Those two fools..." She lets the smoke go out through her nose. "I got the worst of them."

"What about Pa? My pa, Stanley?"

"Stanley?" She crushes her cigarette out in the ashtray. "Stanley was no drunk; I'll give him that much. No, your pretty pa was a *coward*—that's what he was. A coward for leaving you and me. Had he stayed…"

Instead of finishing her sentence, she closes the album and gets up. I watch her as she walks away, toward the kitchen. I open the album and flip the pages, wanting to see Ma when she was young. I recognize her in one of the pictures. She looked real pretty, my ma. She seemed happy then.

13

I think about Stella all the time. Every day I miss her, I want to see her. Though we've met only once, I feel like she knows me more than anybody, like she understands me the way best friends do. At work I find myself wondering what she's doing, where she is, who's with her. In bed I picture us having sex again, laughing and drinking at the same bar, kissing. She wrote her number for me on a piece of paper, which I have right here, in my jeans pocket. Yesterday I called her up from a telephone booth after work. We said we'd meet tomorrow at a diner on Baker Street. I'll tell Candy I have something planned with a few teachers in the evening. She won't suspect anything, I hope.

I'm sitting on the living room couch with a plate of fettuccine Alfredo on my lap. The TV show I'm watching is a repeat, so I'm not paying much attention to the story. Candy's in our room, talking on the phone. She's going out with friends this evening, very soon actually. I'm tempted to invite

Stella over, to be with her just for an hour, half an hour even, but Candy doesn't know when she'll be back, so I'd rather not take a chance. She hangs up and calls my name.

"Yeah?" I ask, chewing my pasta.

"Remember where we put my albums?"

"Aren't they in the closet?"

"I checked already."

"Why?"

"My mom. She's making a scrapbook—God knows why. She wants a picture of me dressed as a cowgirl."

"A cowgirl?"

"On Halloween. Don't ask."

"If it's not in the bedroom closet, it's probably in the other closet, out front. The one over here…"

"Which one?"

"Near our shoes and jackets."

"Next to the foyer?"

Candy walks out of our room, wearing a chic black outfit. Her hair is all tied up in a ponytail, and her lips are blood red.

I watch her put on her high heels. "You look beautiful by the way."

She grabs her purse lying on the hallway table and says, "I really have to run. Can you find my family albums while I'm gone?"

"Yeah."

Candy comes up to me and kisses me real quick on the forehead and rubs my neck. "I'll be back in a few."

She closes the front door behind her while I chew on my final scoop of pasta. At first my plan was to call Stella as soon as Candy was out the door, but now Stella will have to wait.

If I don't search for those albums right away, I'll forget about them, so I open the closet near the entrance. Sitting side by side on the top shelf are three plastic boxes, each one closed with a red lid. The albums aren't there.

Assuming she wasn't thorough enough in her search, I go to our room. Open boxes and papers are lying about in front of the closet. Candy doesn't like it when I put her things away, so her mess will stay a mess. I search and search, but I still can't find her albums. If they're not in our room, then I don't know. What about her dresser? I start with the top drawer and work my way down. To my surprise I find them in the bottom drawer—her albums and mine—under a pile of long-sleeved shirts and bring them to the bed.

I open my album to the very first page. There I am on a swing. And there's Ma squatting next to me, holding me still and smiling, her teeth showing. I was just a baby, too young to realize I had to smile at the camera. I flip the pages. More pictures of me alone, of me and Ma together. She looked so young, so different then, nothing like the version of her in the hospital bed. I see no resemblance between us except our hair and eye colour. I guess Pa and me share the same features: straight nose, big eyes, small lips, dimpled chin. It's just a guess, of course. I close the album and put it back into the drawer, leaving Candy's albums on the bed.

I turn to the mess on the floor, tempted to clean it all up, and then something vaguely familiar catches my eye: a book with a brown cover. I pick it up and run my fingers over it. The cover seems to be made of leather, or something like it, and there's a brown strap that loops around the book to keep it shut. I unstrap the book and skim through it. The pages are filled with Candy's handwriting in blue or black ink, and many of them are dated.

The first entry isn't long. It was written two springs ago, in 1991.

> *My thesis submission date is approaching. Red's convinced I'll pass ("Like you always do," he says), but what does he know about writing a thesis? Part of me is stressing out over it, while another part is thrilled that my long and laborious life as a student is finally coming to an end. It's time for a big change, a new phase—it's time I move in with my boyfriend. I've already started applying for jobs (I even have two interviews at the end of the week). My mind's flooded with thoughts about school and Red, about my future home with Red, my hopefully brilliant career. Sometimes I stay awake at night imagining how magical my life will be. I can't wait to live with you, Red, my love. It's something I've been longing for since childhood, and nothing would make me happier. Nothing.*

I walk back to the bed and sit down with Candy's diary on my lap. I flip the pages, reading snippets of her writing. The moment I come across something interesting, I read the entire entry. At times I feel frustrated, disappointed, yet always anxious, always curious to know more and more about her life, about what she thinks of her family, her friends—me in particular. Here's another entry:

December 11, 1991

*Being a financial analyst has its ups and downs,
like any other job. There's so much work to do,
too much even. At home I find myself reading
more and more (The Wall Street Journal, The
Economist…) just to keep up with financial
affairs, but it'll pay off—I know it will. Plus I
love making money (who doesn't?). Given all our
expenses, Red seriously thought I'd have trouble
saving, but he was dead wrong. I remember
his lectures about the hardships of living
independently. "There's a difference between
textbooks and the real world." "Having a degree
doesn't make you the expert." "It's not 'cause you
studied money that you'll be good at managing
your own." I feel like he underestimated me,
he didn't believe in me. But I'm not angry at
him—not anymore at least. He wasn't trying to
be hurtful or mean. His intentions were good,
and like any good partner he was looking out for
me, preparing me in his own way.*

*Of course, I earn much more than he does, so I'm
paying a bigger fraction of our bills, which I
guess I'm "okay" with—though I sometimes get
frustrated by his terrible spending habits (beer,
junk food, bar drinks, etc. etc.). I'm beginning
to wonder if he should maybe consider a career
change. Something that pays more? I knew that*

*living together wouldn't be the same as living
apart and that it would bring about new factors
to the equation, new scenarios, a few tweaks
here and there. It really is a work in progress. I'll
have to be patient and see where things go.*

I flip to her last entry, which dates back to February of last year.

February 16, 1992

*We had Italian for Valentine's. I ordered
filet mignon—a rare, delicious pleasure! Red
bought me pearl earrings, but I can't say I'm
fond of them (they even look fake! They probably are…). All in all, we had a great time.
After all these years he still gives me butterflies.
He still has the same warm eyes, the same smile
I fell in love with when we were kids. That's
not to say everything's a-okay. In fact we get
along less now (as opposed to when we were
teenagers or even adults living apart). We're
definitely not a perfect couple, but no couple
is—no couple. I know I can be a pain sometimes. I can be pushy too, impatient. I'm just
anxious to do more. There's so much to explore,
so much to experience. It would be a shame to
miss out on Life, the pleasures of Life when
we're still so young, so full of energy. I want
to do things I've never done before: camping,*

skiing, skydiving even! I want to travel overseas. Journey down the Grand Canal in a gondola. Stroll down the Champs-Élysées! But Red doesn't seem interested in any of this. If only he could be more…outgoing? I feel like he has no sense of adventure, or curiosity. Will he change? Should I be worried? I hear the front door opening.

I'll write again soon.

14

After relieving himself in a public washroom, the beggar exits the shopping mall, walks back to his travelling companion parked along the building's wall, and takes out his water bottle. With only a few sips of water left he must go back in. "Gotta go back," he grumbles with a headshake. He opens the glass door of the shopping mall and slowly makes his way across the vast, quiet food court where people can be seen eating breakfast or reading a newspaper at this early hour. He passes a McDonald's, a Starbucks, a Subway before descending a flight of stairs that leads him to the water fountain, which is attached to the wall opposite the men's washroom. Two stationary objects—a white cleaning bucket labelled *Maintenance Personnel* and a pink mop leaning against the wall—are facing him from a corner. Pervading the air is the all-too-familiar stench of vinegar. There's no one else but him in this isolated underground space as he fills his water bottle to the brim. No one who'll ignore him, shun him, regard him with uncompassionate eyes.

When he returns to ground level, he catches a security guard coming his way. Immediately the beggar quickens his pace. There's no use looking over his shoulder; he *knows* the man is on his tail. In less than a minute he's out again, among city buildings and passing cars, among fast-paced workers heading this way and that, always in a hurry. He wonders if he should visit Cormer at the corner of Preston Street. It's only a few blocks away, and there's a chance he'll find him there. He pushes his cart into the sidewalk traffic, standing out like a northern cardinal among pigeons. Minutes later, as he approaches his destination, he sees his long-time friend walking to and fro with a red cap in one hand and a lighted cigarette between his lips. The last time they spoke was at an ATM two weeks ago.

"Cormer."

"Well, what do you know?" Cormer says, shaking his hand. "How've you been?"

"Not bad, not bad at all."

"Could be better?"

"You know the answer to that." The beggar glances at Cormer's cap. "I wanted to stop by and see you, see how you're doing," he goes on. "Feel like taking a break?"

"Sure," his friend says. "Why not?"

They go to the park a street away and take a seat on the closest available bench. Cormer pulls out a pack of cigarettes and offers him one.

"No, I'm all right."

"Sure?"

"Yeah, I'm good," the beggar says, eyeing the pack. "I'm guessing you spent most of your welfare money this month on smokes."

"You know me. Gotta have my cigarettes and booze. Can't help it."

"Did you eat yet?"

"Not yet, no."

"I can give you something, if you like."

"What do you have?"

The beggar heads over to his cart, thinking in the meantime about what to give and what to keep. The least perishable foods are camouflaged by junk while the other foods—the apple and the bread, the banana and the sandwich—he can grab without having to dig them out. He takes the bread and the water bottle and goes back to the bench.

Cormer, feasting his eyes on the bread, stretches his hands toward the beggar. "I owe you one," he says.

"No need to owe me nothing."

Cormer sinks his teeth into the bread. After two mouthfuls he brings his cigarette back to his mouth.

"What about you and your welfare cheque?" Cormer asks. "I'm guessing half booze, half gambling?"

"Less than that. A third booze, a quarter gambling."

"At least one of us is making some improvement."

"Well, that's just it, Cormer—we spend too much of our cash too quickly. I'm trying to save a bit more now, so I have a plan."

"Oh yeah?"

"Maybe I can use my change on pastries and soft drinks, stuff like that. Only my change."

"That's not really a plan."

"Well, it would keep me from using my bills. I want to keep my bills for what's essential. I think it'll help me save a bit," the beggar says with conviction. "And if I don't have enough change, then too bad—no doughnut, no muffin."

"Didn't you try this ages ago?"

"No. You sure?"

"Pretty sure you did. And it didn't work."

"Well, I don't mind trying again; in fact, I tried it this morning. It was hard, though, but I did it. We'll see." After a short pause the beggar changes the subject. "Something nice happened to me the other day."

"What?"

"There was this old lady who offered me her leftover sushi. And then you came to mind."

"Me?"

"Of course you. *You* were the first person to give me sushi. What a marvellous discovery that was! Even now I still remember what it looked like. You don't remember, do you?"

"No," Cormer says. "You sure that was me?"

"Very sure. And I'm glad you did. Life without sushi isn't really a life, is it? Sometimes I wonder how things would've turned out for you and me had we not met."

"You would've found yourself a woman…or not."

"That's not funny."

"We certainly would've had a TV."

"That much I agree."

"Sixty inches," Cormer says, taking one last puff at his cigarette before dropping it. "But everyone thinks about the had-wes, the had-we-nots," he goes on, stubbing out the cigarette. "Had we known our fate back then, we wouldn't have met."

"True."

"We would've done things differently, anything to avoid being out here. But how could we have known? If only we'd known, eh?"

The beggar lowers his gaze but doesn't respond.

"You know what I did the other day?" Cormer asks him. "I went to the cemetery."

"Really?"

"Yup. Hadn't been there in about a year. It was good to go back. It made me feel good. Whenever I go there, I feel as though my parents know I'm coming. From under the earth or somewhere beyond this place they just know, and they're waiting for me," he says, staring at something straight ahead. "It's too bad I don't remember much about them. It's a shame. I guess…maybe we're all like leaves in a way—our memories. All hanging from a tree, bursting with colour, with sunshine, life. But our memories don't last, do they? Most of them don't. We all know it's just a matter of time before the leaves fall off and wither. Before all that's left is a tree with a few leaves, a few memories clinging on."

A few memories, the beggar says inwardly, watching Cormer bite into the bread. "What did you tell them?"

"My parents? The usual. I still ask them if they're all right. I hope they are," Cormer says, uncapping the water bottle. "They both left too soon, didn't they? Pops at fifty, my old man… I wish, I really wish you could've met them. They were good people, my parents. They were kind people," he says. "I made a pact with them."

"A pact? With the dead? Sounds a little strange."

"You know that's not true. In our world, my friend, strange is the new normal." He goes on to say that his parents never travelled much when they were alive, certainly not with him around making trouble. "So I told them to go out there and see the world, all the pretty places; to experience whatever's good, whatever makes them happy. I told my pops I want two things from him in return. First thing I want him to do is read me a story, a children's story, for old times' sake."

Hearing the beggar laugh, Cormer smiles and says, "What? I can't be young at heart?"

"You drink too much. That's the problem."

"Laugh all you want, but I'm not ashamed. Every night he'd tuck me into bed and read me a story. That's a part of my childhood I miss, a part I want back. And then, of course, there's hockey. Going to a hockey game again with Pops, just the two of us. If there was something we often did together, it was that," he says, smiling to himself. "Like it or not, I wasn't much of a Penguins fan. I loved the Rangers, but Pops—Pops worshipped the Penguins, and he'd go wild as hell whenever they'd score. It was something I'd never see him do anywhere else, really. And so while he was there watching the game, I was there watching him cheer, watching his eyes glow."

"What do you want from your mother?"

"Something sweet," Cormer says, turning back to him. "Maple fudge?"

"Why would I want something that bad after I die?"

"*Everyone* loves maple fudge. What's wrong with you?"

"To hell with your maple. The sweet I'm talking about is a Black Forest cake—four layers of chocolate bliss. That's one thing I knew I'd have on my birthday. Mom was the cook, the one with the blue-flowered apron. If only I could have some of that cake again, that sweet cherry filling. Just a piece."

Cormer pauses, clearing his throat. "So that's it, my friend. That's the family pact. And when it's my turn to go, we'll have a reunion back home in our living room, which was our family room. We'll have coffee and some Black Forest cake, and I'll listen to them talk about where they've been, what they've seen. Just the three of us like it once was. It'll be nice. Real nice, I think."

"Yeah," the beggar says, his eyes glistening. "I sure hope it happens." He puts his hand on Cormer's and squeezes it a little. "You know what? I think I'll have a smoke."

Cormer opens his pack.

"Maybe it's time I visit my ma's grave," the beggar adds, plucking a cigarette from the pack in Cormer's hand.

Cormer lights it for him. "There's no better time like the present. Plus you're seventy. Time's running out."

"If only I knew where she was. It's been so long, I don't remember."

"Well, there's always the Internet and the public library."

"Basically everything I hate."

"Tell you what," Cormer says, "if ever you do find her grave, I'll buy you some sushi. How's that?"

"Sounds almost impossible, but sure."

"About ten dollars' worth."

"Don't be cheap, Cormer. I'm in it for twenty."

"You out of your mind? Fifteen, but you have to share. Let's be reasonable here."

They settle the deal with a cordial handshake. A blanket of silence comes down upon them now, enveloping them as they sit there watching the downtown traffic. After a while Cormer, having finished the bread, reaches for the water bottle next to him and brings it to his mouth for one final sip. He's about to say something to his friend, but when he turns and sees him with his head down, his eyes closed, the ash drooping like an arch from his cigarette, he changes his mind and looks away, fixing his gaze on a pair of fallen maple leaves lying motionless over there, across the street.

15

We're in the park, all scattered. Lacey's by herself next to a tree, and there's Mickey close to me but not too close. Finn has the ball between his hands, and his eyes are locked on Cara, who's pinned in one corner of the park, moving left and right. He throws the ball at her but misses. Cara runs after the ball and takes it before Hank does, and now Hank's running backward with his hands up in front of him. Cara knows she doesn't stand a chance against him, so she lets him go. I'm near the flat-stone mound, away from all the action. I run over to where Lacey is, keeping my guard up. Meanwhile Cara targets Rex. She throws the ball too high, but Rex tries to catch it anyway. The ball slips out of his hands and falls to the ground. Cara runs off all proud of herself, and I'm happy for her and even happier that Rex won't win. The last time we played dodgeball he won and made a big scene about it. If only Hank and Finn could lose, too. Mickey has never won at dodgeball, so if it comes down to me or him, I'll let him win on purpose. I hope the game doesn't last too long 'cause I hate dodgeball. Lacey hates it, too, but she doesn't decide what game to play. Either Hank and Finn decide or (if both aren't there) we vote.

Lacey and me run over to the bottom of the bridge. As we do so I see the ball travelling from Hank to Finn, from Finn to Hank—they're trying to get us. They're closing in on us. We're still now, facing Hank and Finn with our backs to the bridge. Finn has the ball. He's close enough to take a shot. If we turn and run to the other side of the bridge, our backs will be exposed, so the only option we have is to move sideways. I think I can save Lacey by shielding her while she goes under the bridge to the other side, but Finn doesn't give me a chance to tell her anything. He throws the ball at Lacey with all his might. It travels so fast I don't have time to protect her, to prevent the ball from hitting her face. She starts crying. Hank and Finn just stand there, looking at her. Cara's running in our direction with Mickey not far behind.

"Why did you throw it so hard?" I shout.

Finn says nothing.

"You're a fucking ass!" I tell him. "She's not your size! You're just too dumb to understand that!"

Cara's with her now, talking to her, trying to calm her.

"What did you say?" Finn asks, moving toward me with Hank by his side.

I don't budge, I don't look away, but I want to run. I want to run away 'cause I'm scared, but I won't 'cause I'm angry. I'm too angry.

As soon as we're face to face Finn pushes me and says, "Don't you call me dumb again, you little shit."

"See what you've done?" My voice is breaking. Lacey's still crying. "You hit her in the face and didn't say sorry. Say you're sorry, then, if you're not an ass!"

Finn doesn't say sorry. Instead he pushes me again, and I push him back and shout, "Say you're sorry! Say it!"

Hank pushes me to the ground and now Finn's on me, slapping me while Hank's pinning my legs and Finn…he's hurting me he's too strong and I can't fight back I can't I just can't, and now the tears are coming they won't stop coming and the girls are shouting Leave him alone! while Mickey's on his knees behind me covering my face with his hands and shouting Stop it Finn! Stop it! Stop!

"Little prick!" Finn says, and lets go of me.

He gets up and Hank frees my legs. Before they leave, Finn kicks my leg while I'm still on the ground, breathing hard.

"Keep crying, dumb-ass," Hank says.

"Yeah," Finn says, walking away with Hank. "Fucking wuss."

Mickey helps me up.

I'm sniffing my snot and wiping my tears, looking down at the grass, breathing hard, and I say, "I'm fine…I'm fine."

"Let's go away. Let's go over there," Cara says, pointing at the little mound on the other side of the bridge.

The four of us don't speak as we make our way to the mound. Once we get there, I turn around and see Aaron, Alf, and a few others (but no sign of Hank or Finn) walking around and talking near the main mound.

Cara asks me if I'm all right, and I tell her I'm fine, even though I'm not.

"We should talk to their parents," she says.

Lacey shakes her head. "I don't know... What if they're grounded and hurt you again?"

I don't answer.

"If they can't watch TV for two weeks, they'll think twice about hurting him," Cara says to Lacey.

"We can tell their parents that," Mickey says. "No TV for two weeks; otherwise they'll keep picking on you."

"Let's just forget those assholes."

"But they didn't say sorry, Red," he says, taking his glasses off, wiping them with his shirt. "They didn't say it."

"Well, it's not like their sorry means anything anyway."

"I'm sitting down," Cara says, and like a row of falling dominoes we all sit down after her, first Lacey, then me, then Mickey.

It doesn't take long before we stop talking about what happened earlier. None of us wants to play anything, so we're still on the mound, away from everyone else. Lacey's plucking at the grass on my right, Cara's making little braids with Lacey's hair, while I'm busy chatting with Mickey about the worst school subjects, about the games we play at recess, our past teachers.

Our conversation ends when we hear a distant voice shout, "Cara! Supper's ready!"

"I'll be back," she says, and off she goes, running to her backyard door.

I'm tired of sitting, so I lie down instead, feeling the grass poke at my back and arms. I look up at the white of the clouds and all the colours behind the white. Mickey and Lacey lie down, too, and Lacey says she wants to go back to school in September. I don't want to, but I don't tell her that. Mickey agrees with her.

"Next year I might go to Disney World," she says. "I've never been. I really want to go."

"I want to go, too," Mickey says.

"What's there?"

"Lots of fun things," Lacey says. "Games and fireworks. Waterslides."

"It must be expensive, though."

"Yeah. I wish we could all go together—you, me, Mickey, and Cara."

"My ma wouldn't let me."

"Why not?"

Lacey doesn't know Ma's poor. (She doesn't know that I rarely go to birthday parties 'cause Ma has no money to spare for presents. Or that my clothes are second-hand, or that some of my toys were bought at a garage sale.)

"I don't know. I have a feeling she wouldn't let me."

Hank's voice reaches our ears.

"Not him again," Mickey says.

"If he wants us to play dodgeball, I won't," Lacey tells us. "I won't. I'm scared, Red."

"Then we won't. We don't need to play anything with those two pricks if we don't want to."

I turn myself over and look around. There's Lacey's mother standing on her balcony. "Lacey, your mother's there."

She gets up and gives her mother a shout. Her mother waves at her to come in.

"I gotta go, but I'll be back after supper."

She runs off and goes in through her backyard door.

Mickey's still lying on his back with his hands on his chest like a mummy, not moving.

"Mickey?"

"Yeah?"

"You going somewhere tomorrow?"

"No."

He yawns, and then I yawn. Filling the air is the smell of cooking meat. Neighbours are coming out onto their balconies one by one, turning on their barbecues. Soon Mickey's mother will open the balcony door and shout his name.

"You want to do something tomorrow?"

"Okay," he says.

"Mickey?"

"Yeah?"

"Thanks."

"For what?"

I'm having trouble saying what I want to say. It's not something boys tell each other, even friends. Maybe that's why it's still inside me, inside my mouth.

"For what?" he asks again.

"For helping me."

But that's not what I want to thank him for. I wait a few seconds and try again.

"You're...you're the best, Mickey. My best friend."

16

You okay?" Stella asks up ahead, among the trees.

I nod, dragging my feet up the slope.

"Need a break?"

"A break wouldn't hurt."

I never thought I'd be so tired and out of breath from walking and jogging. Maybe it's me—maybe I'm just out of shape. Our date started this morning. We jogged from her place to a Lebanese restaurant she wanted us to try downtown. After lunch we each got ourselves a water bottle, then set out for Mount Ashmore. We've been hiking up the mount for God knows how long now. Seems like we've been here all afternoon.

"I can see you're tired," she says, handing me her water bottle.

"Let's find a bench. No slopes."

"Don't you wanna get to the top?"

"More or less."

I hold out her water bottle, but she tells me to keep it. She takes the lead and for a short while neither of us speaks. Now and again I hear branches cracking beneath our feet, people shouting nearby or far away, movement in the trees. There's so much green. So many shades of green. Some of the leaves have so much light on them they look golden, even yellow. The roof of green high above us has thousands and thousands of holes in it, all different from each other, all showing bits and pieces of the sky.

"If I'd known better," I say, panting, "I would've bought myself two water bottles."

"Well, you *did* pour half of yours all over your face."

"That wasn't very smart of me."

"And you also drank the other half in two or three gulps—just saying."

"I don't see myself doing this kind of thing ever again."

"But it's so much fun!" she says. "If I had to choose between this and biking or training, I'd choose this."

With my legs moving less and less from exhaustion, the gap between us widens. Stella turns back to join me, closing the distance. I wrap my sweaty arm around her shoulder, drawing her to me. There's something about this place—maybe the trees or maybe the feeling of being enclosed—that makes me think of my childhood.

"It's strange," I say.

"What is?"

"I'm having these flashbacks all of a sudden."

"Good ones, I hope?"

"Good and bad. A lot of bad, actually."

There's a bench up ahead, unoccupied. As we walk toward it I squeeze her shoulder. Without slowing down, without saying anything, Stella looks up at me. Her brown sunglasses are giving her eyes a mysterious quality, making them look like two dark shadows in a haze of brown. I watch these shadows dart from my eyes to my lips. I lower my head and kiss her.

"Tell me," she says.

"It's nothing, really."

"Sure it is. I wanna know."

"I'm not so sure where to begin."

"Well, what were you thinking about?"

We finally sit down on the bench. No words can even describe how relieved my legs feel.

"A park. That's what this place reminds me of. It was called Emerald Park, and we were about a dozen altogether— all neighbourhood kids. In the summertime we'd meet up in the park and play these games. Have you ever played kick-the-can?"

"Never," she says, shaking her head, and so I explain the game to her.

"It wasn't an actual *can*?"

"Always a soccer ball. And there was this girl I really liked. My first crush. She'd often hide in the bushes. Sometimes I knew where she was hiding, but I wouldn't always call her out. That's how much I liked her. I'd think about her all the time; even at the dining room table I'd see her face in my soup."

"Did she like you?" Stella slides her sunglasses up on her head.

"Yeah. She told me so once. I had two good friends at the time. She was one of them. I didn't really like most of the others, though. They picked on me, made me feel like an outcast. But they were kids anyway, and you know how kids are. I thought maybe they didn't like me 'cause I was poor and not from the same block.

"I kind of wonder sometimes what they're up to, if they've changed and all. There was this one kid who was older than all of us. He told me something once, something I still remember to this day: He said I was good for nothing. That—that really got to me. See, I was never school smart, and my ma couldn't afford things like hockey practice or piano lessons and whatnot. And I never finished high school. I have no talent in anything. Nothing unique. As much as I hated that kid, he was right when he said that to me. Good for nothing—those words hurt me more now than they did back then."

I unscrew the water bottle and take a long sip.

"I'm sure that girl you liked would've disagreed with you on that, like I do."

I manage a small, crooked smile. After a brief moment I say, "You know, there were times when I'd act real silly. I wanted to do what everybody else did on weekends. Like family outings. One of my friends would often go to the beach. So sometimes I'd pretend I was there, too. I'd fill my bathtub with water and pretend I was swimming in the ocean, floating in the water with my face to the ceiling."

Seeing her smile, I go on: "And there was this one time when I stuffed my school bag with some snacks and a flashlight. Every now and then my friend would go camping for a few days. So one afternoon I set off to the park with my school bag. And there I was, crouching in the bushes, pretending I was in a forest somewhere, on a secret mission. I had a lot of time to spare, but I sure was creative."

"I think it's nice," she says, giving me a nudge on the shoulder.

"What about you? What was your childhood like?"

"Oh, gosh. My childhood… I'd say it was normal."

"That's it?"

"Boring, in a nutshell. My neighbourhood was nice and quiet. I made very few friends there, so life got pretty lonely. That's it, I'm afraid."

"I don't buy it," I tell her.

"What? Why?"

"A pretty girl like you must've had a boyfriend."

"Oh, God, no."

"You didn't have a boy crush?"

"No. Well, maybe."

"Who was he?"

She takes the water bottle from my hand and finishes it.

"A boy from the neighbourhood," she says, rising. "He was really cute, too."

I tell her I want to know more, but all I get in return is a no and a bit of laughter. We resume our trek up the mount. For a while we don't talk, we just walk. At some point we over-hear a group of hikers discussing TV shows up ahead. That's when Stella breaks the silence. She fills me in on her top five TV shows. As much as I want to listen, my mind is still fixated on my childhood friend—her shiny hair, her chocolate eyes, her lips coated with pink gloss. Stella would've liked her, I'm sure. They would've been good friends back then. Best friends, maybe.

"You know what I mean?" Stella asks.

"What?"

"About books."

"Sorry, I missed a few parts."

"Still tired, aren't you?"

"Yeah."

"I was saying that if I had to choose between the book and the show, I'd definitely choose the show."

"Me, too."

"I don't know how people can read eight-hundred-page books without getting bored. I'd lose my mind after page fifty. Even a show can be a lot. The more you get into a show, the harder it is to stop."

"Relationships are kind of the same when you think about it."

"Yeah?"

"Well, the longer you're in a relationship, the harder it is to end it," I explain. "It's the investment. A time and feeling investment, if you know what I mean."

"Like you and Candy—Cara."

"Yeah." I frown. "Like me and her."

IN LESS THAN FIFTEEN MINUTES we find ourselves walking up a flight of steps that leads us to the top of the mount. When we finally arrive, we make our way to the lookout area. Anchored to the ground are these huge owl-like binoculars along the railing. About a dozen people are there already, taking pictures or admiring the view.

"Isn't it beautiful?" Stella asks, her hands gripping the railing.

"It is."

I'm standing behind her, our hands intertwined, my face hovering over her shoulder. Unable to see Stella's face, I suddenly picture her as my childhood friend, and my grip on her hands tightens a little.

17

When the beggar wakes up from his nap, Cormer is gone. His water bottle, half full more or less, stands upright on the bench while his cigarette, unfinished, lies on the ground near his shoe. He rises to his feet and puts the bottle back into his cart. With hunger gnawing at his stomach, he searches for his bag of mixed nuts. He finds it under a box and pulls out a handful of cashews and almonds, which he devours at once. To keep himself from taking more, he covers the bag with layers of junk and sets his cart in motion.

So far this morning he's made quite a bit of change, more than enough to buy himself something warm and crispy, an apple pie at McDonald's. Wouldn't that be nice? he thinks. Picturing himself relishing the taste of those apple slices, the irresistible texture of that crust, he quickens his pace resolutely. He would've asked Cormer to accompany him so they could share the apple pie, but when he gets to Preston Street he doesn't see him. He walks on until he lands on Milton

Street, where he recognizes the signature yellow *M* sticking out among sun-blasted trees.

It doesn't take long before he finds himself there, under the *M.* The beggar opens the glass door, expecting to go in right away. He doesn't. Four customers are coming out. Three of them ignore him while the last one says, "No money. No," with a quick headshake. The beggar watches them go, searching for a letter that would best suit each of them. Maybe an *E?* he thinks. Or a *D?* Neither, he tells himself, stepping inside. Four lousy *C*s.

The air is cool here, refreshing. The customer service area is up ahead, populated with self-service kiosks and only one short lineup instead of three or four at this hour. After joining the line as customer number five, he checks the menu board hanging from the ceiling, his eyes straining to read the words, the prices. Everything is more expensive, even the beverages.

His gaze shifts from the menu board to customer number three before him. She steps forward beside customer number two, but her voice is so low the beggar can't hear her. Judging by her profile, he figures she's no more than twenty. It's only when she turns to face customer number four that the beggar notices the listlessness in her eyes, the pallor of her face, her frailness.

She shows the customer her hand, which has a few coins in it, and says, "Sir…I was wondering if you could help me out. I don't have enough for an apple pie. Just fifty cents, sir. That's all I ask."

The man shakes his head.

"I'm hungry, sir."

But all she gets is another headshake, another no. Her last resort is standing two paces away, and yet she doesn't acknowledge him. She's about to return to her spot when he calls out to her, twice. Only then does she walk up to him.

"Excuse me," the beggar says, observing the track marks on her arms, "I couldn't help but overhear. I don't have much, but if it's the apple pie you want, I can help you buy one."

"That would be great, sir."

"Stay right here with me."

He dips into his pocket for loose change, which the girl notices immediately. She puts her money back into her pocket.

"It'll be all right," he assures her. "Stay right here."

The man serving alone at the counter is a skinny, bespectacled blond with the name tag, *ERIC*, pinned to his shirt. His co-workers are moving back and forth behind him, performing different tasks. Two or three minutes later it's the beggar's turn to be served.

"I'll have two apple pies."

"Anything else?"

"That'll be all."

"Actually," the girl chimes in. "I'd rather have nuggets if you don't mind."

"Nuggets?"

"Yeah. A box of six."

Her answer catches him off guard. He asks Eric how much six nuggets cost.

"Four ninety-nine."

He hesitates, his heartbeat quickening. "All right. All right, then."

"One apple pie and six nuggets," Eric confirms. "That'll come to seven forty-six."

The beggar sets his coins on the counter, then takes out the rest of his pocket change. Casting a side glance at the girl, he says, "Your change?"

"My change? Oh, yeah." With feigned surprise, she slowly produces her quarters and nickels and dimes.

"That's four loonies," the beggar says. "Four…four quarters, three dimes, another dime—that's…"

He's trying to add up the amounts but keeps blundering. It's her sluggishness, her unwillingness to help, he tells himself. Annoyed, unable to concentrate, he turns to Eric for assistance, his sweaty fingers tapping the counter.

"You have seven twenty-five," Eric tells him. "Twenty-one cents short."

"Twenty-one cents," the beggar repeats after him. My bills, he thinks, touching his front pocket. I could always use one of my bills, but I'd rather not. "I guess…well, maybe…maybe you can make an exception?"

For a moment Eric just stares at him with his mouth open, motionless as if in a trance. The suspense makes the beggar uneasy. He's about to get his wallet when Eric answers, "Yeah, that's fine," and starts collecting the coins.

"YOU'RE A LIFE SAVER," she says, already chewing as the beggar returns to his cart.

Without wanting to, he looks down again at those ugly track marks, which are even more noticeable now under the sun. "Will you be okay?"

"Yeah. We've had worse days than this."

"Who's *we?*"

"My boyfriend and me. Anyway, I gotta get going." She backs away, turning to leave.

"Where you headed? I'm off that way, too."

"Why do you want to know?"

"Just asking." He improvises a lie: "Besides, I have nothing planned."

"I can see that."

The beggar frowns. "Well, I like taking walks. If you don't want to, that's fine. I'll run along and leave you to it."

She watches him take a bite of his apple pie. He's about to push his cart when she starts mumbling to herself.

"What's that?"

"I said, 'All right, fine.' Two blocks, but that's it. I have things to do, you know. Places to go."

IN NO TIME AT ALL they get to a less crowded street where they're greeted by a row of benches along the sidewalk. The beggar, enjoying a second bite of the apple pie, asks her where she's from.

"Here," she says, tossing the empty nugget box on the ground.

"What neighbourhood?"

"Weston. It's a poor neighbourhood, south of here."

"Weston... Oh, I've been there a few times. It's nice and quiet. People keep to themselves."

"Yeah, it's a pretty qu—"

A vibrating noise interrupts her. "Sorry," she says, sliding a cellphone out of her front pocket. "Hello...? Where are you?

You said we'd meet at McDonald's... What do you mean you've used it all...? Fuck, you're an idiot, Sam. I bought that with *my* money...! Fine, I don't care... I said I don't care! Keep your money! Where the fuck are you...? You better still be there, you hear me?"

She hangs up and puts the cellphone back into her front pocket. "What an asshole."

"Sam's your boyfriend, I assume?"

Instead of answering his question, the girl says, "Do you use? Do you have anything I can—?"

"No drugs in my cart," the beggar replies matter-of-factly as they stop near a shaded bench. "You mind if we sit down?"

"I'm not sitting down. I'm going."

"Where? To that Sam of yours?"

"Why do you care? You don't even know me," she says, and walks away.

"Guess I don't feel like eating the rest of it!"

She stops and turns around. "What?"

"This," he says, shaking the apple pie in its box. "Don't feel like eating it anymore."

The girl goes up to him as he settles himself on the bench. "Give it to me, then," she says. "If I sit down, you'll give it to me?"

The beggar nods, and so she takes a seat next to him with her hand lying half open between them, waiting for it, study-ing him.

After a brief silence he says, "Believe it or not, I wasn't always wretched like I am now."

"That's pretty hard to believe."

He almost laughs. "Well, it's true."

"You had an addiction."

"What?"

"*You*," she says, her bluntness stinging him like a needle prick. "You had an addiction. Didn't you?"

Why? That's none of your business, *I did, yes, I did*, how dare you, how can you be so rude? he thinks as he sits there, glaring at her, stiffening from the sting.

"I don't think you should... I mean, it's something I... I'm sorry."

"For what?" she asks, moving her hand a little closer to his on the bench.

Just as he's about to respond, someone in sports gear zips past them, back forward, feet going in perfect circles. The beggar, watching the front and back wheels recede among the cars, squeezes the box he's holding and says, "God, I miss it. I miss my bike."

"Your bike?"

He nods. His eyes light up. "My childhood bike," he says. "It was the best—best thing I ever got... It's a shame I lost it, though. I shouldn't have. But yeah, we had good times together. Great times, going places... I miss it."

He pauses, only because he needs to blink, and lets out a stifled laugh. "You know, I wish I could travel anywhere. Even now, at my age," he says, hearing the wind behind him. "Like a lake somewhere... Someplace calm and sunny, always calm. Away from everyone."

"So why don't you?"

"Sorry?"

"Why don't you go? I mean, no one's making you stay."

The beggar pulls himself up, leaving the apple pie on the bench. "I guess you're right," he says, glancing at her, and walks back to his cart a few metres away.

The girl, raising her voice, asks him, "Do you have a cigarette?" but receives no answer. With his hands grasping the cart handle, the beggar looks down and sees the ghost of his old beloved bike in profile, floating toward him over the sidewalk.

No, he won't turn, *She's watching me, she's still sitting there, isn't she?*, to look at her, to say goodbye. Nor can he go, his mind won't let him. The sight of his bike so close to him, so remarkable there, on his canvas, leaves him unsatisfied. He wants to shake his head as if to say, No, it's not enough. There's more to view, he tells himself, assessing the scene like a painter. The bike alone won't do.

Time, as if it could suddenly read his mind, ceases for a moment. Things around him begin to blur. Then magically, with the stroke of his brush, the ground beneath his feet morphs into lush grass. A bike path unfurls itself before him like an endless scroll. Mounds of green, bursting with dandelions, take shape. As he puts the finishing touches on the canvas—a few bushes and trees here, a few children there, running—the beggar pushes his cart forward, toward home. His little slice of paradise.

18

Justin needs help painting his new home," was my excuse this time. Candy seemed indifferent to it. Maybe that's because she, too, has plans of her own today—plans that don't involve me. In order to be with Stella, I've been deceiving Candy using an imaginary bar friend called Justin. "Justin's moving soon and needs help packing," "Justin needs help unpacking," or "We're fixing things in his basement." So far Justin's been a huge helper, the best weekend excuse in my current situation.

Stella's staying with Kimiko, a friend from school. Kimiko's off to her boyfriend's cottage for the weekend, so Stella and I have the apartment to ourselves. I'm not sure how long we'll stay today, but I like it, I like everything I see. Each room is painted two different colours, which I find kind of weird, in a cool way. One of the walls in the living room has a built-in fireplace. All the browns and greys of the décor, the furniture, the floors—all of it gives the apartment a warm, rustic feel. Kimiko seems to have a thing for plants. She has pots of them, pots of all shapes and sizes, in every room. I'm staring at one right now in Kimiko's bedroom, where Stella and I have just made love. I'm lying on my side, facing Stella, watching her rest. She has one leg over the blanket, the other underneath it. I place my hand on her bare leg and run it up to her waist. Her lips start to curl; her eyes open.

"Stop," she says, smiling more and more as if she's about to laugh, but I don't obey. My hand goes up to her breast and stays there, cupping it gently.

"You wanna eat something?" she asks, turning on her side to face me.

"Chocolate?"

"Umm…not sure about chocolate. But Kimiko has this really delicious blueberry pie."

"I'd like that."

She slips out of bed, puts on a thin white robe, and disappears into the kitchen. I drop my arm down the side of the bed, not looking at the floor, just letting my hand move about in search of my underwear.

"What do you want to do?" she shouts from the other room. "Oh, and before I forget, do you want milk? Tea? Coffee?"

"Coffee sounds good."

"And my first question?"

"Umm…" I'm still in bed, slipping my underwear on, thinking about what to say while I hear Stella opening a cupboard, then the fridge. "Don't know. We can do nothing."

"What's the fun in that?"

The kettle is humming its tune. I finally get up, but I don't leave the room. I go to the desk by the window. Two piles of books stand on opposite corners of the desk. In the centre there's a closed Hilroy notebook labelled *Kimiko*, with an HB pencil resting slantwise on it. Kimiko must've written a lot because the pencil tip is almost flat. I open the notebook and start reading the first line, then the second, until I reach the middle of the page.

"What are you doing?"

I close the notebook and look out the open window.

"You were reading her short story?" she asks, curling her arm around mine. The kettle is getting noisier.

"It was just lying there. I couldn't help it."

She picks up a book from one of the piles and reads the title out loud. "*The Castle*. Haven't read it, but apparently *The Metamorphosis* is phenomenal. Have you read it? *The Metamorphosis*?"

What is she talking about? I shake my head.

"What about this?" She swaps *The Castle* for the next book from the same pile. She opens the book to a random page.

"'He was unlike anyone she had ever known,'" she reads. "'It was not his outward beauty she was jealous of, for it was inferior to her own. It was his splendid mind, his acquired alphabet she wanted most. With time he had reached the letter *V*; he had achieved something only a select few could do. Oh, but wouldn't it be nice, she thought, watching him read, admiring his curiosity, to have his empathy and awareness, his mastery of German, his sense of control? What if I reach the letter *M*? she thought, rolling her sleeves as she returned to the kitchen. She would be more than satisfied. She would even settle for *H*.'"

She looks up at me and says, "I have no clue what this means. It's not even interesting." The kettle is screaming. She puts the book down and rushes out of the room.

Unlike Stella, I think I know what the author means. It's about knowledge and experience. Newborn babies have neither, so they would be ranked *A*. The more knowledge and experience people acquire, the further they advance down the alphabet. The character is ranked *V*, and because most people don't have this rank his mind must be splendid. Secretly I'm glad it makes sense to me but not to Stella. I doubt even Candy would understand it. If I had to choose a rank for myself, I'd choose a letter like *F* or something. There's too much I still don't know about the world to be even halfway down the alphabet. I'd give Candy a *K*, but because her mind isn't all that splendid she doesn't deserve a *V*. She's not open-minded, not empathic, not supportive of what I do, so *K* it is. Stella may not be a *V*, but she's more than a *K* to me.

"Milk or sugar?" Stella shouts.

"Both."

I put my clothes back on and leave the room, feeling uplifted. Stella's putting away the sugar. I help her bring the coffee and pie into the living room. I'm moving slowly, careful not to drop the fork or spill any coffee on the floor.

When we're both seated, I ask her how long she's known her friend Kimiko.

"Since university," Stella says, changing position.

She's facing me with her back against the arm of the couch, her left leg bent like an *L* on the seat cushion between us. She blows into the mug and takes a quick sip. The coffee has too much milk in it for my taste, but I don't tell her that. Instead I say, "I think it's pretty hard to keep in touch with anyone from school. People get so caught up in their first career job, or their new life somewhere, like in a different city and all. It's only natural for them to move on, leave their old friends behind."

"I'm definitely one of those people," she says. "I've kept in touch with no one except Kimiko and two others—that's it. We have a rare bond, the four of us. We used to go on these amazing trips together, and we were roommates for three years—that's how inseparable we were. The best trips I ever had were with my gals. Like in Paris."

Stella gets up and puts the mug on the coffee table and picks up the plate of blueberry pie. Rather than sitting back down she kneels before me.

"I remember the smell of pastries everywhere I'd go, not to mention the chocolate éclairs," she says, going on about the raspberry tarts and crème brûlées she tasted, the cobbled side streets "no lady should ever cross in high heels," and a place called Montmartre.

She sets the plate on the coffee table and turns to me with animated eyes. If I were to look away, she might think I'm not listening when I am, so I can't even reach for the pie I still haven't tasted but want to.

"Montmartre's my little slice of paradise. It's actually a hill, a magical place—not at all like what you find here, in Willobrooks. I swear my heart must've stopped beating when I saw the Moulin Rouge."

"What's that?"

"The world's best cabaret," she says.

I nod without saying anything.

"There's this incredible red windmill on the roof, with tons of lights built into the blades. I never went inside the cabaret, but seeing those blades at night, all illuminated, gosh…"

Now she's talking about how dazzling everything looks there. From one house to the next the shutters are a different colour, she says. The flowers are red and blue, yellow and violet in pots, on windowsills, hanging from windowsills. Even the walls, she says, are anything but grey or orange, and "some have ivy that climbs all the way up to the rooftops. I remember taking a small white train that went through narrow streets and brought me to the very top of the hill where the basilica is—I forget the name. The view from up there was so breathtaking I went back there twice, and I can't wait to go back again."

Within seconds her enthusiasm dies down, her eyes dim. She picks up her plate and sits back down on the couch, her left leg bent in the same position as before. "Sorry. I'm really sorry."

"What for?"

"I got carried away. I get excited just thinking about places like that."

"Yeah."

"You would love it there. We could go together."

I'm not quite sure what to say.

"Wouldn't you want to go?"

I press my lips together and nod. It really does seem like a nice place, Montmartre. Listening to her describe bits of it the way she did made me forget the pie, even the coffee in my hands. I found myself understanding only bits of the bits but wanting her to go on, to make me imagine a world different from my own. Right now I don't have that want feeling. I'm not interested anymore in all that Montmartre talk a minute ago. I think it's strange how feelings can change so quickly.

To be honest, I wish she hadn't brought up Montmartre in the first place. Why didn't she talk about something I know or some experience we both shared? We could've just eaten the pie in silence, glanced at each other from time to time, I don't know. Leaning forward, I swap the coffee for the pie on the table, waiting for her to speak again.

"Is it good?" she asks, nudging my thigh with her foot.

"Yeah. It's good."

Her ankle bracelet catches my eye. It's a short chain of little hoops, golden like the colour of her skin, and glazed. Hanging from one hoop is a starfish. I didn't notice the bracelet earlier while we were in bed.

"That's nice."

"This?" She brings her foot closer to herself and touches the bracelet. "I got it a while back."

"It's not something you see a lot, even on women's feet."

"Maybe. I've got tons of ankle bracelets back home. They're a fetish of mine. That and shoes."

"I'm guessing you chose a starfish bracelet 'cause you like the beach."

"Exactly."

"I've seen a bracelet like that before, but I don't remember where or when," I tell her, observing her expression.

"So what do you want to do after?" Stella asks, and takes another bite of her pie.

I lay my hand on her leg and bring it down to the bracelet. My fingers are now interacting with the starfish, flipping it over and over.

"You're making me think of..."

"Of?" she asks.

"It's nothing. I was... I need to buy some salmon at the grocery store."

"We can do that."

She takes her leg off the couch and goes back to eating her pie.

WHEN I ARRIVE HOME IN THE EVENING, I find Candy sitting cross-legged in bed, with papers around her. I walk into the room and say hi to her. I kiss her on the forehead. She doesn't kiss me back.

"What did you buy?"

"Salmon. A few other things."

Her eyes return to her papers. I leave the room without another word. Entering the kitchen, I hear her say the words *why* and *take* but nothing between the two and nothing after *take*. I put the grocery bags on the floor and head back to our room. This time, I don't go in. Her head turns; her eyes look up at me.

"Why didn't you take the car?"

"What?" I ask, thinking about what to say next.

"To see your friend Justin? I'm just wondering. You never take the car on the weekends."

"No, I take the subway."

"That's kind of strange. I mean, you have a car, *my* car. Why would you take the subway?"

"Well, you said it—it's *your* car, not mine."

"You know what I mean."

"We've been living together for two years, Candy."

"So?"

"So it's… By now you should know I like taking the subway. Anyway, you go out, too, on the weekends. If you go out, you'll take the car, not me. Like today."

She doesn't answer.

"Didn't you go out with friends today? Didn't you take the car?"

"Our plans got cancelled," she says, looking less serious. "Anyway…"

She goes back to reading her papers while I go back to the kitchen and pour myself a glass of juice, my hand shaking, my heart pounding.

It was only a matter of time.

19

It's been a full year since we moved in together. To celebrate our anniversary we're having supper at a twenty-four-hour diner. Candy has just opened her present. Judging by her reaction I'd say she was expecting more than a box of chocolates and a bouquet of roses. She didn't give me a wish list, so I wasn't quite sure what to buy her. Maybe everything she truly wants I can't afford—maybe that's why she says, "Don't worry about it," whenever I ask her for gift ideas.

It's my turn now. I peel off the Scotch tape and start ripping away the gift wrap.

"What is it?" I ask her.

She takes a bite out of her grilled chicken. "Open it."

Part of me doesn't want to. If it's something super expensive, I'll feel cheap inside, embarrassed. I open the box and there, staring at me with its black face, its tiny white hands, and silvery ring frame, is a gorgeous men's watch. I grab it by the scales of its metallic band, turning it this way and that, admiring the details. I tell her it's too much.

"But do you like it?"

"Whether I like it or not is—"

"Red," she cuts my answer short, "do you like it?"

"Very much."

"That's all that matters, then." She raises the glass of vodka to her lips, still looking at me.

"It must've cost you a fortune."

"If you say so."

To please her I unclasp my outdated watch and try the new one on. It really does look nice around my wrist; for once I'm wearing something flashier than all the jewelry on her body.

"Thank you."

She smiles as I bring her hand up toward me and kiss it.

"We've come such a long way," she says, her face animated. "It's already been a year. Can you believe that? Seems like much less to me."

"For sure."

"Remember the day we moved in? I do. You were right, you know."

"About what?"

"Me, of course. The soon-to-be financial analyst, fresh out of school. That's who I was when we moved in. Never lived on my own, never had bills to pay, never had to cook, etcetera, etcetera. I was inexperienced, and I knew that. But look how everything turned out for me. It's not as bad as you made it sound. I save every month; I go out with you, with friends. I even travelled to Fiji. You were so sure I'd be short on money, but I wasn't. It was manageable in the end, and it still is. Even you're better off now than before the move."

"I only wanted to prepare you."

"I know. But the point is, we're doing pretty well."

"*You want us to go on a trip?*" *I ask, trying to guess what she's getting at.*

She sets her knife and fork on the table. "*If that's what you want, I'm totally in, but it's something else.*"

"*Okay?*"

"*I'm thinking maybe we're ready,*" *she says.*

"*For what?*"

"*To have a baby.*"

"*A baby?*"

Her eyes are beaming. "*Wouldn't that be wonderful? I mean, we've been together for a long time, and we've been living under the same roof for a year. It wasn't always easy, I admit that. But I honestly feel like we're in a pretty good place. A happy place.*"

I nod.

"*It's not that big of a surprise, though,*" *she adds.* "*It's something we've been talking about since high school. The difference between now and then is that now we're ready. I know I am.*"

Am I truly ready? I ask myself, looking away from her. Am I ready knowing I'll be spending more and saving less? Shouldering more responsibility? Sleeping less? Despite all the challenges, I really do want a child, a junior version of us. Someone I can always be there for, someone I want to see grow and learn, become something. I'd be a happier man. A better man, I think.

"*I don't see why we can't try.*"

"*Really?*" *she says, grinning.* "*I know we can do it, Red. We'd be such great parents, you and I, and I mean that. You know how much I want one.*"

"*Yeah.*"

"*If it's a girl, let's call her Sally. And if it's a boy, Charlie.*"

"*You realize that your life, the things you love doing, will be put aside.*"

"Not everything."

"No trips. No shopping sprees, no—"

"I know. I know that, Red. But I want this."

Our waitress comes by to check on us. "How's the food?" she asks.

"Marvellous," Candy says. "I've never been happier. Say, do you mind taking a picture of us?"

Candy reaches into her purse for the camera. I get up and go to her side of the booth while our waitress positions the camera for the shot. As soon as I'm seated I wrap my arm around Candy's shoulder. She leans in and whispers, "I love you," in my ear. I kiss her, and together we turn to face the camera.

"Okay, love birds, on the count of three: one...two..."

I love you, too, Candy.

20

Ma's been working since nine this morning, so I'm alone at home with my toys for company, and when I'm alone for too long I get bored. Like today. Biking gives me something nice to do, something I never get bored of. So far I've had my bike for a year and it's never let me down. I take good care of it like a baby, and above all it's blue, my favourite colour. I got it for free. There was this woman, one of Ma's co-worker friends back then. She was doing a big home cleanup, getting rid of her son's things, including a bike. Ma thought of me and brought it home for me to keep. It's by far the best present I've ever had.

I take my bike out of the apartment. Before I do anything else, I lock the door behind me—Ma's orders. With the key in my pocket, I get out of the apartment building and hop on my bike. The sun today is so strong I have to look at the road with eyes half shut. In seconds I reach the street where the dépanneur is. The street is pretty busy at this hour—cars are coming and going non-stop, people are entering and leaving shops or restaurants, some are chatting, smoking alone on the sidewalk next to a door, waiting in line at the bus stop for the 53 with a book in their hands, a cigarette in their mouths. I see couples, too, having an afternoon drink at Vivienne's, a café I've never been to.

The dépanneur isn't busy, though. I think I'm the only customer there. Tony's the owner, and he's known me since I was very little. His belly always sticks out of his undershirt. Right now he's sitting on his wooden stool and reading the newspaper.

"Redmond," he says, putting his elbows on the counter. "Doing well?"

"Yes, Tony."

"How's your mother?"

"She's good. She gave me some money."

I reach into my pocket for the coins and lay them out for him. There's a see-through covering on the counter, and underneath it are columns and columns of lottery tickets with cool art on them.

"Let's see here."

He counts the money and says I can pick ten pieces. The candy jars are stacked along the wall next to the counter. Each jar has its own kind of candy. I don't want each kind. I want only three: the race car (Ma says it's something called toffee—what is that anyway?), the sour cherry, and the fuzzy peach.

"I'll take four race cars, three cherries, and three peaches."

Tony uses a long metal tweezer to get them out and puts them into a brown paper bag for me. He knows I prefer the race cars, so instead of picking four, he picks a whole bunch of them—how many I can't say. I thank him 'cause he's real nice. Before I leave he says, "Say hi to your mother for me, okay?"

"Okay, I will," I tell him, even though I won't.

Mickey and his family are spending the entire day at the beach. He invited me to come, but I said no. I would've said yes, but I can't swim. I can't. And I'm not sure if I want to know how. People choke or drown, and I wouldn't want to be one of those people. I wonder what Lacey's doing. Maybe she's home. I could always ring at her door, but there's a chance her grumpy father will answer it. When I get to the park, no one's there. I lean my bike against a tree and sit down in the shade. I pop a race car into my mouth and look around, hearing myself chew.

Very soon I hear something else. A door opening. I turn and see Lacey waving her hand at me from her balcony. She takes the stairs, and now she's out of her backyard, running toward me with her hair flapping and her hands dancing in the air.

"What are you doing?" she asks, and sits on the grass beside me, under the tree.

"I'm eating my candy. Want some?"

"Okay."

I pass her the paper bag and tell her she can take what she wants.

"The sour cherries are so good," she says.

"Yeah. They're real good."

"The race cars are okay."

I put the paper bag between us, and she takes another sour cherry.

"Cara thinks you like me," she says. "Is that true?"

How does Cara know something like that?

"Maybe. I don't know."

"You're a boy and you're my friend. So that makes you my boyfriend, right?"

"That's very strange."

"It is?"

"Mickey's not my boyfriend. And Cara's not my girlfriend."

"That's true," she says. "Can I ask you something else?"

"Yeah."

"You have secrets, don't you?"

"I guess so."

"Like what?"

There's a fallen branch with a leaf attached to it next to me. I take it and use its tip to drill holes in the earth. While I do so, I try to think of a secret.

"It's a tough question."

"Well, I have a few secrets," she says. "Me and Cara—we share secrets."

"Me and Mickey don't do that. We play games."

"Maybe that's 'cause you're boys. Boys keep things inside."

"Maybe, yeah."

No, that's not true. I tell a lot to Mickey. (He knows Ma's a drinker. He knows I don't have much of anything. Plus he knows I got four Cs on my report card this past June.)

"I have an idea," Lacey says.

She gets up and tells me to stay put, not to move a muscle. She goes back to her backyard, walks up to her balcony, and disappears behind the door.

I wonder what she's doing, what's taking her so long. I'm glad that we have the park to ourselves—that I have her to myself. Lacey comes out holding a metal box and runs toward me, smiling, and sits down again at the exact same spot. She gives me the box. It has a pale pink cover, with blue waves, yellow hearts, and orange diamonds along the edges. In the middle there's a flower made up of red and purple petals, some close together, others spreading out a little.

"It's mine," she says. "I got it at a flea market."

I tell her it's real pretty, and she takes it back.

Why did she say *flee*? Or did she say *free*? Maybe she meant some other word 'cause *flee* and *market* don't go together.

"I got it last year, for a dollar. I've been keeping it in my drawer, not using it for anything. But then I thought about something the other day. I thought I'd bury it out here, in the park."

"Why would you bury something nice?"

"I saw someone do it in a movie. There was a girl who buried a toy in the ground, and only she knew where it was, so it was safe."

"I don't know, Lacey. I wouldn't do that to one of my toys."

"Well, in the movie, the toy in the ground turned into a big magical tree. But it's just an idea."

She opens the box. There's a keychain inside—a purple bunny all sparkly under the light. She takes it out for me so I can see it better, then puts it back into the box. There's also a pencil and two sheets of fancy paper, with different kinds of flower drawings at the top. She starts writing on one of the sheets. I watch her and wait, feeling a bit confused, a bit curious. But I'm definitely more confused than anything else.

"There," she says, and hands me the pencil and the other sheet of paper. "Now it's your turn. You write down a secret."

Before I write anything down, I read her secret: *I have a berth scarre on my but.*

"You have a scar?"

"Yeah. I can't show it to you, so you'll just have to trust me. I also have beauty marks on my arm, but the scar is a better secret."

What about me? Don't I have beauty marks, too? I could always write *I have more than twenty beauty marks on my body* or *I once peed my pants at school*, but they're not secrets I want to share. After a while I find something and write it down. I give her back the pencil and sheet of paper. Lacey reads my secret out loud, but I don't think she likes it 'cause she says, "Is that really a secret?"

I nod and say, "It's what I want."

"My parents aren't so happy these days." Lacey's folding the papers now, looking a bit sad. "They fight a lot."

She places everything in the box, then puts the cover back on.

"Come on," she says, and steps out of the shade.

I follow her, and when she reaches the bushes (the ones near the bridge), she kneels down and says the earth here is easier to dig into. We dig together, and I feel the earth filling itself under my nails. We make a hole in the earth big enough for the box. I place the box in the hole, and together we cover it with the earth we just dug out.

She turns to me, still on her knees. "You won't tell anyone about this, will you?"

"No."

"Swear?"

"I swear, Lacey. I won't tell."

"I won't, either," she says. "It's our little secret."

21

I have a soft spot for sunsets. Sometimes when I'm down I look up at the sky, at those sunset colours all dreamy and serene. After a while something extraordinary happens: All that negative energy boiled up inside me begins to shrink, until it's all gone. Until I feel a certain lightness in my veins. Sunsets are kind of like an egg cooked sunny side up. The sun is a punctured, bleeding yolk, and the colours of the blood leaking out, spreading out across the sky, are never quite the same from one day to the next. Right now the clouds are milky grey and purplish, with streaks of pink here and there along the edges. The view is not as stunning as those you come across on the highway, but it's definitely a sight worth seeing.

We're eating sundaes on a pier at the Old Port of Willobrooks. I'm leaning against the rail with my sundae cup hovering over the water. The wind is alive and kicking.

"Would you have wanted a brother? Or a sister?" Stella asks out of the blue, her hair flapping behind her like a flag.

I dip my spoon into the ice cream, then the chocolate syrup.

"I would've wanted a brother," she continues. "A little brother, much younger than me so I could spoil him."

"A sister?"

"Not so sure. Something tells me we wouldn't have gotten along. You know how girls can be: jealous, competitive, among other things."

Twisting my body toward her, I see in the distance a large boat sailing across the water. Half a dozen people are in it, some of them waving. On the pier, couples are moving past us in opposite directions. There's a flock of white birds near the edge of the pier, pecking at bread crumbs or pasta—something white.

"The answer is yes for me. Yes to a brother."

"I was expecting a no," she says.

"Really?"

"Just kidding. Honestly I wasn't sure."

"I would've wanted an older brother. Someone to look up to, other than my ma. She struggled a lot, her whole life. I can't imagine what she would've done with two kids."

"How was she like? Your mom?"

I turn around so that my back is leaning against the rail. Stella doesn't move. She's hardly touched her sundae.

"Kind. She was kind, my ma. And she was real gentle when she wanted to be. She was also a sad person, more often than happy. A sad day was a grey day, that's what I used to call it. She'd have many grey days, and then a yellow—or a happy—day would follow, just like that. You could never tell when that yellow day would come. It seemed kind of random to me at the time, but on those days I'd see the best of her glowing."

Stella smiles, her eyes shimmering. Because of the wind she has a band of hair plastered to the skin under her nose.

Ma, I tell myself. I want to see you, Ma. I want to know if you're okay. I want to tell you things I never had a chance to say. I wish you were here. I wish.

"You okay?"

"Yeah."

I get off the rail and turn around. I feel Stella's arm wrap around mine, her head gently touching my cheek. I slip my hand into my pocket.

"Here."

I give her my sundae cup and open my wallet. The picture is still there, behind my debit card. I show it to her. It's a picture of Ma and me in a photo booth. We were both smiling—or maybe not. She was. I had my mouth open, and my eyes were real big, full of awe.

"That was a while back."

Stella turns the picture around and says, "Red, age six," and flips it over. "You look very…awake."

"I don't have many pictures of us, but this one I keep with me as a good luck charm."

"You're definitely hers. You have her lips. Her nose, too. Her bone structure."

"I'm glad to hear that."

She hands me back the picture. "She was beautiful."

"Vicky," I say, looking at the picture one more time before putting it away. "Her name was Vicky."

SHORTLY AFTER NINE O'CLOCK I get back to my apartment. The door is locked, and I can hear voices—not just Cara's—coming from inside. I reach into my front pocket for my keys, but as soon as I pull them out I hesitate. I don't want to go in, I tell myself as I bring the key up to the lock. With a deep sigh, I open the door.

"Ah, he's here," Cara says from either the living room or the dining room.

She appears before I get a chance to remove my shoes.

"What's going on?" I ask.

"Elena's here, with her husband," she says. "Where were you?"

"I was doing overtime." I keep my voice low. "Why are they here? I thought they were coming in a few months?"

"What do you mean 'Why are they here?' Elena's my friend," she's whispering now, "and they've come all the way from California. They chose to come earlier. What's wrong with that? Honestly, Red. Honestly! And all this overtime? It's too much. It's not helping at all."

"Cara, there's nothing I can do."

"Just come in," she says harshly. "They're waiting."

"Is everything okay over there?" Richard asks.

"Yes!" Turning to me, Cara says, "We're eating," and leads the way to the dining room, where our guests are sitting opposite each other.

They're eating lasagna, and they each have a glass of white wine next to their plates. The bottle, almost touching Richard's glass, is a bit more than half full.

"Elena, Richard, this is Red."

"Cara said you were doing overtime," Richard says. "You must be hungry."

"Not really."

I take a seat opposite Cara. I glance at Elena, then at Richard, smiling nervously.

"I'll just have some wine for now," I add, and pour myself a glass.

"Cara's told me a lot about you," Elena says. "I'm glad we can finally talk face to face."

I'm trying to find something polite and fitting to say, but nothing comes to mind. The fact that they're all staring at me doesn't help at all. I can't think anymore. Too many eyes. Too much attention.

"Red's a little shy, as you can see," Cara jumps in. "We were talking about their plans this week."

Richard wipes his mouth with the napkin. "Yeah. We were thinking about visiting the Old Port tomorrow."

"That's a good place to start," I tell them.

Richard and Elena are like night and day. Richard has dark brown eyes, almost as dark as his hair but not as shiny. The top of his head makes me think of waves in the moonlight. Elena, on the other hand, has blonde hair and pale blue eyes, and unlike Richard she doesn't wear glasses.

"So Cara told me you work at an elementary school?" Elena says.

"Yeah. It's not far from here. I get there on foot."

"He might not stay there, though. Not long-term," Cara says, loading some food onto her fork.

"I like it. I like my job."

"Well, it's a start," she says. "Red might go back to school."

"Really? That's a bold move," Richard says.

"I'm not sure about that," I tell him.

Cara's eyes are on me. "But it's something you're considering."

"I'm happy doing what I'm doing."

"That's great," Richard says. "That's the most important thing."

"And money," Cara says, looking at him, then at me.

After a short but awkward silence, Elena asks me if I have any hobbies.

"I like to bike a lot."

"Richard's into stamps. And coins."

Richard clears his throat. "Just a few of those childhood obsessions that never died out for me."

Cara swallows her food and says, "Red also spends time with his friend on the weekends doing I don't know what."

I'm about to take another sip, but I put the glass back down. "Well, if I stay here with you, I'll hear you complain about why we don't go out as much and why I'm still a janitor, why I'm not something you want me to be, or why I watch too much television and blah, blah, blah."

"You're exaggerating."

"Of course I am, Cara. Of course."

I excuse myself, hoping she doesn't do the same. I walk to the living room and open the balcony door. A hot breeze brushes my face as I step out onto the balcony. Richard comes out seconds later and offers me a cigarette. I take one from his pack, and he lights it for me before taking one for himself.

"Women," he says, half smiling.

"Yeah." I turn to him, but I don't return the smile. "Women."

He leans forward against the balcony rail and, raising his head a little, blows out a pale cloud of smoke. I step forward, put my free hand on the rail at arm's length from him, and exhale deeply. We don't go back in. We finish our cigarettes right here, in the moonlight. Exhaling. Gazing out on the evening scene and listening. Keeping our thoughts to ourselves.

22

Mickey won the rock-paper-scissors match. I was hoping to lose anyway. Mickey was so relieved when I was rock and he was paper. (Like me, Mickey hates being the seeker.) My loss was Hank and Finn's victory. They laughed at me, called me names, like they always do. I'm with Mickey on the main mound, and there's Cara, talking to Rex. Her tone of voice tells me she doesn't agree with him on something. I catch Lacey staring at me on the deck of the bridge. I don't know how long she's been staring, but I'm glad she is, I'm very glad. She's on her knees, and her arms are folded, resting on the rail. She puts her finger up to her mouth like she's hiding a secret. (She *is* hiding a secret.) I give her one of my happy faces, then look away, at the soccer ball moving back and forth under my shoe. When I look up again in her direction, I still see her there, staring at me.

"All right, shit face. Start counting," Hank orders.

Finn comes up to me and smacks the side of my head.

"What was that for?" I shout.

"Keep your fucking eyes closed," he says, and walks back to the base of the main mound where Hank is waiting for him.

I close my eyes and start counting. Alf giggles somewhere to my left, Hank shouts for no reason, and now I hear them running all around me on the grass, on the paths, so many steps that fade and fade until all that's left in the air is a whisper, a soft swishing sound, coming from the trees.

When I reach twenty, I open my eyes and turn around. Still counting out loud, I run toward the street. I don't care if they catch me cheating; I just keep running, not looking back. I step onto the neighbouring block and follow the path between the grass, hearing no one, thinking only about the girl I'm going to meet under a tree.

The others can't see us 'cause we're hiding behind a row of townhouses. Together these houses act as a huge wall along the block. Next to this wall are mounds and trees and a few paths like the one I just took to get here. I'm walking on the grass now. Lacey's kneeling under the tree with her butt almost touching her heels, and she's plucking the grass. She looks up at me before I get to her.

"Did they see you?" Lacey asks.

"I don't think so." I duck under the tree branches, all leafy like in a jungle, hanging low. I kneel beside her so that we're eye to eye. She laughs.

"What?"

"I can't believe we just did that," she says. "They must be wondering what's going on."

"Probably."

"Did you tell anyone?"

"Only you."

I hold on to a few grass hairs, but I don't pull any out. We're so close I can smell her. Maybe it's the T-shirt she's wearing or maybe it's her hair or something she put on her skin—whatever it is, it smells nice. We don't say anything. (What if she's trying to? I know I am.) I don't want her to get bored, but I can't find anything good to say.

"Red?"

"Yeah?"

"Have you ever—?"

Voices stop her. We can hear them—Hank and Finn, Rex and Alf. Hank's calling me names again: "Red, you asshole! You stupid idiot!" Me and Lacey are staring at each other with our eyes and mouths wide open, listening.

"Where the fuck are you?" Hank cries out.

"Rrrred! Rrrrrrred!" Aaron and Alf shout, one after the other.

And now it's Cara's turn: "Lacey! Lacey, come out! Come out!"

I start laughing. Lacey does the same. She's covering her mouth with her hand as if she's afraid they'll hear her somehow.

"Do you think they'll find us?" she asks.

"No. They think we're hiding on their block."

"I'm not sure if this was a good idea. If Hank and Finn see you…"

"I'll run as fast as I can. I hope it's Hank."

"He's almost never it."

"I want him to be. That'll teach him."

The yelling has stopped. I wonder what they're doing now that their seeker can't be found. I tell Lacey, "I'll be right back; I'm just going to spy on them for a second." She wants to come, but I don't want her to get caught or be seen with me, so I tell her to stay put.

I step out from the tree and head to the last townhouse at the end of the wall, near the middle of the block. The bushes along the side of this house are as tall as I am. My arms are stretched out in front of me, my hands are pushing leaves away from my face and now I'm part of the bushes, breaking branches, making the leaves talk. As soon as I reach the other end I stop moving. I check what's happening. He's there, I see him now. Standing alone on the main mound with his head down and his foot on the soccer ball. He's it, he must be. I want to laugh real loud so he can hear me. I want him to know he lost and I won. Next time I hope Finn's it 'cause he's just as mean as Hank. I turn back when Hank sets out for one of the alleyways. I run across the grass and duck under the tree leaves again, breathing hard.

"What's wrong?" Lacey asks.

"Nothing. I was right all along." I kneel down next to her.

"What happened?"

"Hank's it."

She puts her hand up. I put mine up, too, and we give each other a high-five. I'm glad she's on my side. I'm glad Mickey is, too. 'Cause not many people are.

"I want to go there and kick the ball."

"Don't be silly," she says.

"I want to. I might. Just for the fun of it."

"He'll hurt you."

"I'll run."

"I don't think you'll do it. I don't want you to."

Maybe she's expecting me to give her an answer she wants to hear, but instead I wait for her to say something more. She does.

"Have you ever kissed a girl?"

I'm confused. I thought she'd say something like, *Don't go, Red. Please don't go.* Her question has nothing to do with what we're talking about, and I'm not sure I even want to answer it. I've never been asked something like that before. At school, nobody talks about who they've kissed, and I've never seen any of my friends kiss anyone except on the cheek. Maybe Lacey means on the cheek. Ma's not a girl, though. I guess she doesn't count.

"Yeah," I say.

"Really? Who?"

"Well…there's my ma."

"Ewww. I would never do that."

"But she's my ma. It's on the cheek."

"That's not what I meant. I meant on the lips."

"No, then."

"Never?"

I shake my head.

"And you? Have you ever kissed a boy?"

"Once."

That's not the answer I wanted to hear. "Do I know him? What's his name?"

"Why?"

"What's his name?"

"Are you jealous?"

Yes, I am. But Ma always says if you don't want to answer, don't answer. I look down at the grass.

"You're jealous, aren't you?"

"Never said that."

"If you like me a lot, you'd be a bit jealous."

I pull out some grass hairs next to my knee, picturing a lip kiss. I think it's kind of gross if you ask me. I don't understand why she'd do something like that. She's not a grown-up. I hope the boy she kissed isn't someone I know. Part of me doesn't want to find out.

"Do you like him?"

"He's nice. He gives me candy."

"He's your boyfriend, then."

"No."

My heartbeat goes back to normal. I'm still a bit shocked about the kiss. Half shocked, half curious. I ask her if she liked it, but she doesn't answer right away. She starts playing with the grass hairs in her hands. Maybe that's her way of telling me she's thinking. Finally she says, "It was weird at first. But I liked it." She stops for a second or two and then asks, "Do you want to kiss me?"

I look away. It's not a question you should ask someone. Kissing should just happen, I think. My heart's beating faster again.

"Do *you*?" I ask.

"I asked you first."

"I don't know."

"All you need to do is close your eyes, Red. Close your eyes."

I close my eyes, but as soon as I do I want to reopen them. I force myself not to. My heart's beating even faster now. I can't help it 'cause I can't see what's going on, what might happen, so I just wait. I wait and I try not to move. And now I hear her and the grass stirring I want to open my eyes, but I can't, I won't, and now our lips are touching I lean a bit forward so our lips touch even more and I'm kissing for the first time we're kissing with our mouths closed, and just like that my eyes open and there she is so close to me her eyes are closed and then our lips part. She gets up and steps out from the tree. I step out, too, after her, and now we're walking side by side across the grass, still hidden behind the townhouses.

"So? You liked it?"

I nod.

"Really?"

"Yeah."

Looking back, I kind of wish it had gone on a little longer. Maybe our tongues would've kissed, but that's something only grown-ups do.

The mound we're on has a big rock in the centre of it. We lie down shoulder to shoulder on the slope of the mound, facing the clouds. Our hands are so close they almost touch. Almost. I wonder if she liked the kiss as much as I did, if she likes me more than a friend likes a friend. Should I ask her?

"Lacey…"

"There's an alligator in the sky."

"Where?"

"There," she says, pointing her finger somewhere to my left.

I focus on the shapes. I see an ugly *L*. Is that what she's talking about?

"I see an *L*. No alligator."

"It's there. It's moving real slow. Why are clouds so slow? Do you know?"

"Maybe they're just floating. Like on water."

"There's a bird over there," she says, pointing her finger at something above the wall of townhouses. "If I could be an animal, I'd be a bird."

"Not me."

"I'd fly, that's why. I'd travel everywhere, like a magic carpet. Wherever I want."

"I think I'd be a dog."

"That's good," she says. "You kind of look like one, too."

"If I was a dog, I'd protect you and Ma, 'cause that's what dogs do. They don't run away and hide when something bad happens. They help out, and they're fast. Hank and Finn would be no match for me. I'd run after them and bite their legs. They'd never mess with me again." I turn to her. "I'll go back and kick the ball."

"Okay," she says, and we both get up from the grass. "I'm coming, too."

"You can come with me to the bushes, but you'll stay on this block."

"I'll run with you."

"No."

"I want to run with you."

"I'll kick the ball and come back, okay?"

"Okay."

We go to the bushes. I go in first, parting the branches and leaves for her, and when we reach the other end, we crouch and look into the distance. There's Finn, talking to Rex near an alleyway; Alf and Aaron are sitting on a rock not far away, poking the earth and talking, while Cara's walking by herself, looking around like we are. Hank appears out of an alleyway and walks up to the main mound.

Lacey and me step back behind the bush leaves. Mickey and a few others are still hiding, but I'm not going to wait until they're caught. My hands are starting to sweat a little. Hank won't let me get away with it. He'll hurt me if I kick the ball. But if I don't go, I'm not the dog I said I'd be, and dogs aren't wimps. And now Hank's moving toward the bridge; it's hard to see where he's going exactly. He's out of sight. Maybe he's heading to an alleyway, or maybe the bushes or the other side of the bridge, I don't know. But the courage in my heart pushes me out of the bushes. I'm running now with everything I've got. No one can stop me, nothing can slow me down, not even the wind. Their eyes are all on me; Alf and Aaron are cheering me on, shouting, "Red! Red, kick it! Kick it!" I feel like I'm running a marathon. Here comes Hank, my evil competitor. Here he comes on the other side of the bridge, running fast, screaming, "Hey! Hey, you asshole! Don't you kick it! Don't you dare kick it!" But it's too late. I kick the ball and head back, running as fast as I can. The captives are fleeing, too, finding a new place to hide, and I can hear Hank and Finn screaming my name, but I don't look back. When I get to the bushes on the neighbouring block, Lacey isn't there. I run back to the tree where we kissed. She's there, sitting under it, waiting for me.

"I did it, Lacey! I did it!"

"I know," she says, and gives me a high-five. "You were fast."

"What are you guys doing?" Cara asks, running toward us. We don't answer.

"I was looking all over for you, Lacey. You were here all this time? With him?"

"Yeah," she says.

"What's wrong with that?" I ask.

"You're not allowed. It's against the rules to leave the park."

"I don't care about the rules. It's just a stupid game, that's all."

"Then why do you play? If it's stupid?" she says in an angry tone.

"Just leave him alone, Cara. It's not a big deal."

"Well, that's not what your mom thinks. She's been calling your name every minute. It's past six, Lacey. You were supposed to go eat ten minutes ago. I told your mom you were hiding and that I'd find you."

Lacey steps out from the tree and heads off home, with Cara by her side.

"I'll wait for you here, Lacey."

"She's not coming back, Red."

"Lacey?"

"She's not coming back," Cara says, louder this time.

Still walking, Lacey looks at me over her shoulder and smiles.

23

We're eating outside, not too far from home. It was my idea to go out for lunch, and so here we are at Florence, Baker Street's most popular bistro. The scrambled eggs I ordered aren't all that great, but the bacon and French toast are pretty good. Cara's eating a chicken Caesar salad. She must be real hungry because she's eaten about half of her salad already, while I'm only a quarter of the way into my meal. It amazes me that so many people choose chicken salad as a main course when all they get are two, maybe three, strips of cold chicken and too much lettuce.

We're sitting in a corner of the terrace, exposed to the sun. A family of four beside us is preparing to leave, while two couples behind Cara have just taken their seats, and there's our waiter, serving pancakes and fruit at another table.

"They liked you," she says. "Elena and Richard."

"Yeah." I stop chewing and swallow. "Did you invite them to come yesterday? Or did they invite themselves without telling you ahead of time?"

"I knew they were coming."

"You knew, but you didn't say anything."

She doesn't respond.

"Why didn't you tell me?"

"'Cause," she says, chewing her salad. "'Cause you would've spent the whole evening elsewhere, on purpose. You would've gone to a bar or some other place. I know you."

"Maybe I should have. I would've been spared all that talk about…"

"About what?" she asks, cutting a chicken strip in three. "About your work? That it might be temporary?"

"Why would you say something like that?"

"Why wouldn't I? It's possible."

I don't think I'll be finishing my meal. I'm not all that hungry anyway. I put my fork down, distracted by everyone around me. Stella's off somewhere with her friend Kimiko. I wonder what they're doing. Maybe they're at a restaurant like we are, having a nice conversation—would they be talking about me?—or maybe they'll go shopping later, go to a spa or do some other activity girls love to do. Wherever they are, I'd rather tag along with them than sit here with my own girlfriend.

"I'm surprised you suggested we eat together," she says.

"Why's that?"

"Well, it's Saturday. And we both know where you go on Saturdays. What's his name?"

"Justin."

"Yeah, him."

"He still needs my help with his new home."

"Doesn't he have a family? Other friends to help him out?"

"Don't know, Cara. Just thought I'd help out, that's all."

"What about me? What if I want us to do something? Don't I—? Don't we count, too?"

"Of course we do. But you never told me anything you wanted us to do. How am I supposed to guess?"

"I can't tell you anything if you leave in a flash. You tell me you're leaving right before you step out the door—right before. You're not being fair."

The look I give her puts an end to our discussion.

Cara wipes her lips with her napkin and gets up. "I'm going to the washroom," she says, and takes her purse along with her.

Watching her leave, I can't help but wonder how much longer my Justin excuses will last. Every time she mentions him, every time we talk about him, I feel vulnerable, a bit antsy. I'm not good at improvising answers, and if my answers aren't convincing enough, she'll smell the lie and get the truth out of me. I'll have to find something else to talk about before she gets back—anything to keep her mind off my weekend dates.

With so much movement happening in every direction, my eyes can't stay still. They dart from table to table on the terrace, from pedestrian to pedestrian on the sidewalk, and finally to the other side of the street, which happens to be less crowded for the time being. By the door of an empty store sits a homeless man with a sleeping bag rolled up beside him. I watch him disappear and reappear with every passing car. He looks tired and broken, his clothes soiled and torn. His lips seem to be forming the same words over and over as people approach him. No one stops to give him some change.

He must be starving, I tell myself, reaching into my pocket for money. I check the coins in my hand, trying to determine how much I'd be willing to give away, and that's when I hear her calling my name. It never occurred to me that she'd be right here on Baker Street, of all places. I look up, wishing she were far away at the moment, wishing the voice were not hers, but there she is, all smiles. The person standing beside her must be her friend Kimiko.

"Stella. What are you doing here?" I ask her, checking to see if Cara's coming.

"We're gonna do some shopping this afternoon. It was Kimiko's idea. Kimiko," she says, addressing her friend, "this is Red. Red, Kimiko."

We shake hands, and then Kimiko says, "Stella's told me a lot about you."

"I'm sure she has."

Kimiko's much shorter than I expected. Her skin is a flawless pale colour, and her glasses are so big they make her face look too small, even cartoonish.

Stella glances at Cara's plate, and I say, "Cara. She's here. She went to the washroom."

"Okay," she says, turning to Kimiko. "We've got a lot to do, don't we?"

"Here she comes," I tell Stella.

Cara returns to our table with question marks in her eyes. Before she sits down, I introduce her to them.

"Red never talked about you before," Cara says, glancing at me.

"Stella's a friend."

"I work at the school," Stella tells her. "I teach history."

The fact that Cara and Stella are eyeing each other makes me uncomfortable. I'm about to tell Cara that they're off to do a bit of shopping when she says, "I think I've seen you before."

"Really?" Stella asks.

"Yeah. You look familiar."

"We won't keep you from your meal any longer," Kimiko says, grabbing Stella's arm.

"Lots of shopping to do," Stella says. "It was a pleasure meeting you, Cara."

"Likewise."

"Okay." Stella turns to me. "Bye, Red."

And with that, they leave; they're already gone.

Cara, pushing her plate to the side, seems to have lost her appetite.

"What do you want to do?" I ask her.

"I don't know. She's pretty. The tall one."

She's waiting for a reply, but I don't give her one. I put my wallet on the table and set my eyes on the waiter, who's picking up plates of unfinished food. With all of his attention fixed on those plates, he doesn't notice me waving at him as he steps off the terrace. Cara takes her wallet out, too.

"Do you talk to her a lot? Stella?"

"Not much, no. Are you still going to eat your salad?"

She shakes her head.

"All right. I'll take out, then."

As soon as the waiter returns he catches my hand signal. Cara asks for two bills.

"We'll take both meals to go," I tell him, and off he goes with our plates.

"What do you want to do?" she asks me.

"Watch a movie?"

"No, I'm not in the mood."

She's looking over my shoulder, her eyes focused, preoccupied. I wouldn't be surprised if she's thinking about Stella, or about me and Stella chatting at the school, having lunch or coffee together. Stella's lie, at least to me, sounded believable. I just hope Cara doesn't call the school and ask about her. If she's suspicious, she might. And if she does, I wouldn't know what to say.

"Now that I think of it, I need some new makeup. If you want to go home, you can take the car and I'll walk home. Unless you want to come?"

"I'll walk home. You take the car."

After paying our bills in cash, we both go our separate ways. With the bag of leftovers swinging constantly under my arm, I cross the street and make my way to the homeless man. There's a cup in front of him with some money in it. I grab a bunch of coins from my pocket and drop them into the cup without counting the amount. The sound of metal clashing on metal makes him look up.

"You're good. Too good, kid," he says. "Much obliged."

"Here's something else." I offer him the bag of leftovers, which he takes willingly, with a toothless grin.

I notice he doesn't have a fork. "I don't have a fork," I tell him. "I'm real sorry."

The man laughs and says it's not important. And as I'm about to turn he waves at me and wishes me a good day. I set out for home feeling a bit different—something better than good, something I can't really explain—but I like it. I cross the street, smiling to myself.

24

The beggar's moving his grocery cart down a slope, away from the downtown clamour. Though he's not exactly sure which way to go, his gut tells him he must head down and eventually turn right. At the next intersection, he sees a Salvation Army a block away to his left. Worried that a homeless acquaintance may recognize him or talk to him, he quickens his pace down the slope until he finds himself on level ground. The street sign above him reads Hermann. Hermann? A familiar name, he thinks. It's a long street lined with little antique shops, art galleries, a few bars and restaurants. There's more space to move here, less noise, less human activity than on Baker Street, downtown's principal artery.

He's starting to sweat from all the walking, from the increasing heat, and before long he has to stop and remove his jacket. As he does so two ladies coming from behind pass him. One of them pinches her nose while the other one laughs. "Idiots," he says under his breath, watching them shrink in the distance. He resumes his quest but stops within a minute, in need of rest. He parks his cart next to a bench that faces a pastry shop across the street. His eyes gravitate toward all of those fresh pastries lined up in rows on glass shelves, tantalizing him with their shapes and toppings. Refusing to use one of his bills for a pastry, the beggar settles for his leftovers and takes a seat on the bench.

For some time he just sits there all by himself, savouring the ham and squinting, feeling the sweat on his back, the sun on his face. And then, out of sheer fatigue, his eyes close. At first all he sees is a bright darkness, but then images begin to form, one after the other. Images of a sunny beach with birds on the shore and palm trees, a forest backed by snow-capped mountains, a sailboat riding the waves. Suddenly a stranger's voice brings him back to reality.

"Hope I'm not interrupting your meditation."

He opens his eyes and squints at the person standing before him: a frail woman, bespectacled, with curly grey hair just like his and pink-powdered cheeks. She's looking down at him with a coffee cup in her hand, waiting for an answer. The beggar puts his sandwich on the bench and says, "No, you're not interrupting, ma'am."

"May I?"

He scoots over a little.

"Perfect weather," she adds, placing the coffee cup between them on the bench. "I couldn't stay at home."

"Home. What is home?"

The old lady smiles at him. "Are you from here?"

"I am. I used to live nearby," he says, "a long time ago. I'm only back for a quick visit. It's not quite the same as it once was."

"Not just here—the whole city isn't the same," she says, gazing at the stores opposite them. "At least the local school is still in one piece."

"The one with the orange bricks?"

She nods. "Stuart Nelson Elementary School."

"I went to school there, back in the seventies."

"Sixties for me," she says. "I spent most of my life in a classroom. Taught at a high school for thirty years."

"A great profession, ma'am."

"Not at all."

"I'm sorry?"

"I didn't find teaching all that great, to tell you the truth. The last ten years of my career were flat-out terrible. Every kid had a cellphone. Isn't that outrageous?"

"Very much so."

"It still blows my mind. And it all started with the end of humanity—the Internet."

"Imagine in fifty years, ma'am."

"I'll be long gone by then. Thank heavens."

The beggar snorts and says, "I worked at a school, too."

"Oh, really? What did you teach?"

"I didn't. I was a janitor."

"Ah."

"But I liked it very much. I was good at it, I really was."

"How about school? Were you a good pupil?"

The beggar pictures himself in a classroom he remembers vaguely. "Not really."

"Same here. I was horrible up until college."

"But I wasn't disobedient, ma'am," he explains. "I was just terrible at learning things. Terrible at math, terrible at English, science, poetry, all that boring stuff."

"They're all turnoffs if you ask me. I taught history, and even *that* was a bore. Poor kids. I tortured them all year round with a zillion dates, nineteenth-century battles and treaties, bloody invasions. No wonder they hated me."

"Must've been an awful thirty years, not even liking what you taught."

"Oh, don't get me wrong; I didn't hate my job. In fact, I have great memories of it before the Internet. Before all these dreadful cellphones. I'm sure you do, too."

"I have a few."

"Is there a favourite one, if you don't mind me asking?"

"I don't know. It's hard to pick out one." The beggar pauses for a moment, staring into space. "But if there was something I liked about school, one really good thing, it was lunch hour."

"Why?"

"The games, ma'am," he says. "What were they? Touch football was one, yes. And soccer with a tennis ball. You needed two teams to play them. That's what I loved about them—being part of a team. It wasn't about me against everyone, or me being the outcast either, or the bullied one. I wasn't alone. I didn't feel alone, no. My friends *wanted* me. They wanted me to be on their team. I didn't have to prove anything, be someone else to be with them. It's a nice feeling to have, ma'am, the feeling of being wanted."

"I don't doubt it," she says. "See? Wasn't that hard, was it?"

The beggar watches her rise with an effort. Knowing she's about to leave at any moment, he asks her if she's ever heard of Sunny Street.

"Pardon?"

"Sunny. It's the name of a street I'm trying to find. Do you know how to get there?"

"Of course I do," she says, sitting back down on the bench. "In fact, I was just there the other day."

25

When Cara eats out with colleagues she never comes home before ten, her usual bedtime hour. Regardless of what she says—"No, I'll be back early, I promise" or "I swear, Red, this time I'll only have an appetizer and a drink"—I know she doesn't truly mean it. So tonight I expect to be alone, at least for the next four and a half hours. I enjoy having the apartment to myself every now and then. I get to do things without anyone watching, speak to myself without anyone listening, or do absolutely nothing without being criticized.

An hour and a half ago, while I was preparing my meal, I thought about something of Cara's. I went into our closet and searched for her diary. I had to push aside shoes and shoeboxes to find not one but four diaries. They were all piled up inside one of her blue plastic containers. For now they're sitting along the edge of the dining room table, unopened. In case she *does* come back while the diaries are still out I'll have to be quick.

I locked the front door to buy myself some time, and if she catches me putting boxes back into the closet, I'll tell her I was looking for my album.

Having eaten what I could, I push away my glass and plate and bring her diaries closer to me. I grab the pink one first. On opening it I notice the handwriting of a child, and as I flip through it I also notice pencil drawings and heart stickers, even glitter glued to some of the pages. Unlike the diary from last time, this one has no dates in it. I stumble upon an entry written in purple.

> *Today I was outside it was sunny. Lacey and*
> *me we played together. I told her about Red.*
> *She says she doesn't love him. She is lying. I*
> *hate that Lies I know because when we were*
> *at her house she went in her room and I went*
> *inside and saw all her drawings under the bed.*
> *Some were good and some were bad and one*
> *had Red's name and her name together with*
> *big heart in the middle. Like their marry. She*
> *got mad because I never asked her to give me*
> *permission to look at her drawing but I think*
> *she was shy. And she is scared that I will tell*
> *Red about her that she loves him. Maybe I will*
> *do what Lacey did: Me and Red with a very big*
> *heart. If I go back inside her room I will take her*
> *drawing and rip it. Today I am going outside I*
> *hope I will see ~~her.~~ Red. And I hope he will see*
> *me maybe he is there already. I'm going to go to*
> *check now*

Another entry, written in red several pages later, ends with my name, so I have to read it. I have to.

> *Hank is a bully. Finne wants to be him and*
> *he's a bully to. He copies Hank. They both like*
> *to be in charge. They sometimes are scary people.*
> *Yesterday Red had a fight with Hank because*
> *Hank throwed the tennis ball at him while he*
> *was riding his bike. Red fights back even if*
> *Hank beats him up, and sometimes he pushes*
> *hard and Red starts crying because Hank is very*
> *big and strong and he hits. But still Red is a bit*
> *stupid. He fights back when he knows he's going*
> *to be hurt and lose. He should just run away,*
> *that is what smart people do. And he doesn't*
> *know much any way. Once when me and him*
> *and Micky were outside somewhere I said water*
> *kouenches your thirst and he said what? He*
> *didn't understand that. And sometimes he does*
> *not say things right. I have to correct his words*
> *and he doesn't like that his face tells me so. But*
> *I like his face. I want him to like me. I know I*
> *love Red*

As much as I'm curious about her earlier entries (which seem to revolve around me), what I'm most interested in are her latest ones. Before I move on to her other diaries, I flip to the very last entry.

It's been awhile since I didn't see Lacey. That is because she moved away. It's a bit weird without her in the park. Red looks sad even with Micky around. He should get over it. She won't be coming back so he should accept that instead of being sad all the time. I been speaking a bit with him alone, like yesterday evening. He was drawing things on the ground with chalks. Everyone else was doing something else like playing Frisbee. He didn't say much. But we talked about the blue car drawing he was drawing. I said it was nice and he said thanks and then we talked about our hobbys. Maybe that is what him and Lacey use to talk about to each other.

I saw Lacey last weekend on Sunday at her new home. I think I'm the only who knows were she lives and her phone number. Her house is nice and bigger. She says she is lonely now. Because she has no park to be in and no friends around in the summer. But her room is big and pink and we had fun playing a bord game. She asked me how Red is doing and I said he's doing fine and he's happy. She asked me more about him but I didn't like that so I kept my answers short. I said I don't know if he misses you I don't talk to him much he's not always around.

*She didn't ask me to give her house adresse to
Red, so I was glad. What I didn't like was
when she talked about all the things she did
with Red and Micky together but not with me
invited. She should have invited me to. I am
her friend Why? This hurts my feelings and
even thinking about that makes me hurt and
angry. I don't know why he likes her so much.
She is not that pretty. And also her lips are too
small. She told me when I was at her home
that she wanted me to give Red a letter from
her. I read it. I said ok I will, but I don't think
I will. It is in my room on the bed. It's just a
couple lines about that she misses him and stuff
like that. I think I will keep it for now. Or
throw it out in the trash. He will never know*

The diary on the very top of the pile has a hard black cover.
On opening it I come across an entry that ends with an un-
answered question. It was written a little less than a year ago.

September 28, 1992

*I find it so hard to stay concentrated at work. In
fact I don't want to be there at all. I'm stressed.
Always stressed these days, and still grieving. We
each have our own way of coping with grief, and
while I tend to show my emotions (even when I
don't want to), Red doesn't show much of anything. He becomes more distant and spends more*

time in bars. We haven't been talking much, but it's only been two weeks since my miscarriage and our wounds are still fresh. I'm avoiding pregnant friends and family members. It's not that I don't want to see them, it's that I can't.

I find myself staying at home more often, but for how long…? I keep thinking about the weeks leading up to the loss, anything that could have triggered it, but I can't find any wrongdoing. Wasn't I careful? Why did this happen then? I don't understand. The doctor suggests we wait a while before trying again.

Will we?

Midway into the diary, my eyes settle on the name Sally. I start reading from the top.

March 4, 1993

We're trying again—finally! To tell you the truth, I haven't felt this happy in a long time.

I've already started monitoring myself religiously—my body, my mood—for any signs. I want this so much, more than anything, more than Red does. I'm trying to be patient (and above all <u>hopeful</u>) as we wait for good news.

About a month ago I was at my friend's for her daughter's first birthday. I admit I was afraid to go. I was reluctant but I went anyway, forcing myself to. It never occurred to me that I'd come back home feeling so energized, so determined to make it work.

We bonded, her baby and I. She'd been crying for some time in her mother's arms, but when I took her in mine I sang to her. I lulled her. Just watching her gaze, smelling her skin, wanting so badly to nurse her, nurture her—all of it made me realize how much I long to be a mother.

There's something else I want too, something crucial: I want my child to have parents who get along. As you know, my relationship with Red isn't what it used to be. If I had to rate our postmiscarriage life, I'd give it a six or seven out of ten at most. But having a baby will change us for the better. We'll be happier, and his spending habits will stop. The other day I dreamed I'd given birth to a girl, and her name was Sally—Sally, all wrapped up in pink, cradled in Red's arms right here, in our bedroom. It was such a marvellous sight, a marvellous dream.

I think it might be a sign.

Some entries about me are difficult to digest. The further I read, the more her tone darkens. Her truths are affecting my mood, my opinion of her. I'm worried she'll know something's wrong just by looking at me.

I flip to one of her last entries, which was written shortly before I met Stella.

June 19, 1993

Had a fight with Red yesterday. He doesn't try at all. Sometimes I wonder if he's in love with me, or if he's just in it for the sex (it's been happening less and less…). He's lazy and boring—and he's a janitor. That's my boyfriend in a nutshell—that's the man who ~~will~~ might one day father my child.

He should do something better with his life. Something that gives him a real title, <u>that pays</u>. I told him so, and you know what he said? He said I was a control freak, and that it's always about me! He also said I "bitch" about his work all the time and can never be happy for him. But I disagree, wholeheartedly. I wasn't bitching, Red. I was giving you a reality check! You don't seem to realize I'm the one paying the bills. 80% of them! I'm the one trying to keep us afloat. ME. ~~Sometimes I detest him! Sometimes I want to hit him because I'm so mad. You're useless and pathetic. You should be ashamed.~~

~~Most men are pricks. You, Red, are like most men. I wish I could stop loving you.~~

Her very last entry starts off with *What a day!* on the first line, followed by:

> *It was Red's idea to go out for lunch. We hadn't done that in a while so I didn't object. The day before, Elena and Richard were at our place. We had a great time (joking, laughing, talking about work). And then Red came along and ruined everything. When they were gone we gave each other the silent treatment the whole night. I won't lie, though. I was a touch condescending at the dinner table, but I was mad, what can I say? I was mad at <u>him</u>.*

> *I knew Elena and Richard were coming over that day. In fact I'd known days ago but I didn't (couldn't) tell Red, otherwise he wouldn't have come. I thought maybe he'd be back home at a reasonable hour, but no! For a while I've been wondering why he does so much overtime, because it doesn't make sense. Why so much overtime now??? We hardly even see each other anymore, we just coexist. But maybe there's a reason behind his "so-called" overtime. ~~I want to strangle him. I want to hurt him like he's hurting me and I hate him sometimes. I hate you. More often than not I do.~~*

Lunch was downtown, on a terrace. We had a small argument, but apart from that we mostly ate in silence—nothing surprising really. And then something unexpected happened: when I left the washroom to go back to our table I saw her—this teacher at his school called Stella, who was with her Asian friend. When I came back and sat down I took a good look at Stella. There was something strange about her, and I couldn't tell at first what it was. Maybe strange isn't the right word. Something familiar. Vaguely. I've seen teachers at Red's school, but not her. So she must be new, I thought.

And then suddenly, while she was walking away, everything fell into place. She reminded me of my childhood friend Lacey—someone I haven't seen in ages. It can't be her, can it? There's something else too. Something maybe too distinct to pass as a coincidence: Lacey had three beauty marks on her arm, near her wrist. A diagonal line. I saw the same beauty marks, the same diagonal line on Stella's arm. Isn't that odd? Isn't that a rare trait to share? But why would Stella lie about her identity? Or maybe she and Red are…maybe Red knows, but they're both keeping her identity a secret from me? That would explain his late arrivals on weekdays, even his weekend outings (maybe Justin doesn't even exist!). Nothing makes any sense! ~~He better~~

not be dating her. He better not be fucking her because things will get ugly, I'll make sure of that. She better not be her. Of all the women in this world, please let it not be her.

It's a bold assumption. Maybe I'm just paranoid about Red and her, I don't know. After lunch that day I told Red I was going to shop, which was true, sort of. When Stella and her friend left us, I saw them walk into a shopping mall. I wanted to find them and I did, in a shoe store. I stalked them, keeping my distance. Every time she laughed I got jealous, every time she smiled I wanted to wipe it off her face with soap. The more I looked at her, the more I saw Lacey. One thing was clear: I needed proof, a picture of her to be sure. So the next day I rummaged through my closet and drawers for pictures, but I couldn't find any of her. My oldest albums are at my parents'. I'd have to pay them a visit but I'm just not in the mood. Not now. Red, if you're with her I'll never forgive you. I hope you live a terrible life. I wish you nothing but bad luck. You don't deserve a happy ending. You deserve to be alone.

26

When Ma gets drunk, she says things she'd never say to me, or to anybody else. I stay in my room to avoid seeing her that way. Sometimes I hear her talk to herself or shout for no reason. Once she said that Pa doesn't care if I'm alive or dead and he doesn't love me and I'll never meet him. I was so hurt I cried in my bed and thought about Pa all night. Later, when Ma asked me what was wrong, I didn't hold back. I told her everything, but she said she didn't mean any of it.

Yesterday she came home a bit late. I said, "Hi, Ma," but she ignored me, and after I told her about the drawing I'd made of us, she said, "Not now. Just go to your room. Just go." I figured she'd gone on a date that evening and it hadn't gone well.

The men in Ma's life come and go all the time. It's rare that I get to meet any of her dates. I only know about them 'cause of our supper talks at the table. I wish I were strong enough to protect Ma. Sometimes she doesn't choose the right man for her, and he ends up hurting her and they break up. The last one used to beat her. She'd come home with a bruise on her face, and seeing her in pain would hurt me and I'd get angry and worried. When I have a girlfriend, I won't be a jerk like Ma's exes. I'll take good care of my girlfriend. I'll buy her flowers and diamonds, but above all I'll make her happy.

I haven't done much today. Usually when I stay indoors for too long I get lonely, and right now that's exactly how I feel. Stepping out of my room, I find Ma on the couch with a cigarette in her hand and a cloud of smoke pouring out of her mouth. Three bottles of alcohol are on the coffee table along with her drinking glass, which is almost empty. She turns to look at me as I walk toward the front door. Her skin is pale, and her eyes have no spark in them.

"Redmond," she says, coughing. "What's wrong with you?"

"What, Ma?"

"I told you to clean those dishes. I told you. Why don't you listen when I talk to you? Always hiding in your room, leaving me here all by myself," she says, filling her glass halfway with red wine, spilling some of it on the coffee table.

"I forgot."

"You forgot. You… That's not an excuse. That's not…" She takes a sip of her drink.

I go to the kitchen, expecting her to finish her sentence. She's laughing—why, I don't know. I see four glasses and two plates in the sink. That's really not much to clean. I start with the plates.

"You know, honey," she says, laughing still, "this morning I had a flashback of you on Halloween, all dressed up in that awful costume, the one from last year—or was it the year before that? I must've been drunk out of my mind putting all that makeup on you, 'cause you sure as hell didn't look like a squirrel." She starts laughing again. "You looked like a blob of shit!" She's laughing harder now while I clean the glasses. "And you went trick-or-treating like that anyway. Looking like shit!"

I hear her footsteps approaching. I don't want them to. I want to go away, to avoid her, to be left alone.

"Redmond," she says. "Redmond, honey. My little squirrel."

I'm drying the plates real quick. I still have the glasses to dry, but I'll be quick, I have to be quick. When Ma appears, she stops by the fridge and leans her shoulder against it, the glass of red wine hanging from her fingertips.

"Oh…I'm getting a bit dizzy," she says. "It's been a really long day."

She doesn't know what she's saying. It's still daylight. What she really needs is a nap. I drop the dish towel on the counter and take Ma's hand, pulling it toward me as I walk out of the kitchen.

"What? What do you want to show me now?"

"Nothing, Ma. You're tired, that's all."

We enter her room, and I make her sit on the bed. I put the glass on her night table.

"All right, Redmond. All right," she says while I take off her slippers. She lies down on her side, and I pull the blanket up to her shoulder.

"Sleep, Ma. Sleep, okay?"

"Redmond."

"Sleep, Ma."

"I'm dizzy. I'm so dizzy."

I kiss her on the cheek and watch her eyes close.

"What time is it?" she asks without reopening her eyes.

I don't know what time it is. "I'm going, Ma."

"You're going. You're going? No, don't go."

"I'm going, Ma. Sleep now."

"Don't go."

"Sleep, Ma."

"Okay."

I leave the room, feeling better. I want her to fall asleep soon, so I walk as lightly as I can to the front door. I hope she has sweet dreams like the ones I have. Maybe she'll dream about us somewhere nice, or us travelling the world on a magic carpet—something good. She shouldn't dream alone, so I go back to my room and take my stuffed dog Max with me to her room. I put it on the bed, near her hands.

"Take care of Ma for me," I tell Max, stroking its beige fur. "I'll be back soon."

WHEN I GET TO THE PARK, I spot Aaron and Rex sitting on the main mound, Hank and Finn standing on the bridge. Mickey's nowhere in sight. Lacey isn't there, either.

"Red!" Aaron shouts.

"What are you guys doing?" I ask as he runs up to me.

"Rex got a rabbit."

"Oh, yeah?"

"He brought it out."

His rabbit is very small. I've never seen a real one until now. Its eyes are black and glossy, like two bowling balls. Rex's stroking its back, watching it closely. I get on my knees and run my fingers over its left ear, its soft grey fur.

"Take it," Rex says, removing his hand. "Go on, take it."

I wrap my hands around it and bring it toward me.

"His name's Cloudy."

"That's a strange name," I tell him.

"He's grey, idiot. Grey equals cloudy."

"When people think of cloudy, they think of something bad. I wouldn't call my pet something bad."

"Well, it's way better than your name," he says, and takes back Cloudy.

"What's better?" Hank asks, walking up to us with Finn beside him.

"Cloudy's a better name than Red's name."

"Any name is better than Red's name," Hank says. "What kind of mother would call her child Redmond anyway? A drunk mother."

"Shut your mouth."

"We all know she's a drunk. You said so yourself once."

"No, I didn't, Hank. Don't put words in my mouth."

"Yeah, you did," Finn says.

"I said she drinks."

"She's probably a wild one when she's drunk," Hank says.

My anger is boiling up inside me, and I don't know how long I can control it. I've never bad-mouthed his mother, so why is he bad-mouthing mine? I pretend I'm staring at Cloudy, hoping the bullies go away.

"With a bit of makeup on she doesn't look that bad," Hank says. "I wouldn't kick her out of bed, your mother."

My anger brings me to my feet and pushes me forward. I aim for his face, but my hand strikes his chest instead. He grabs me by the arms and uses his strength to throw me down.

"Don't talk about my ma, you hear!" I yell. "Don't talk about her like that!"

"*My ma! My ma!* Look at him. He's crying!" Hank shouts, and starts laughing.

Rex's smiling, Finn's laughing and I can feel the tears rolling on my cheeks but I'm so angry I'm so sad I can't hold them in I can't stop them. My ma's a drunk. It's not her fault Pa left her, he just did. No one should make fun of somebody like that. I picture Ma sleeping, Ma smiling, Ma staring at me, and I want to cry even more 'cause she's my ma.

"Let's go," Aaron says, taking me by the arm. "Let's go."

I get up, wiping my face, refusing to see their winning smiles, to let them see the hurt in my eyes.

"Go on, girls. Walk away."

"Go back to your mommy. Mommy the drunk."

"*My ma! My ma!*" Hank cries out, and now they're laughing even more as I disappear with Aaron into an alleyway.

When we reach the other side, Aaron asks me if I want to go to his place. "We can watch TV or something."

"Yeah."

"Or you can check out my cards."

"I'd rather watch TV."

"All right," he says as we pass Hank's house.

All of a sudden I spot something on the sidewalk and pick it up. It's a card with Hank's face and name on it.

"That's an ID card," Aaron says. "What are you going to do?"

I look at him and say, "Can you keep a secret?"

"I guess so. Yeah."

"I'm serious, Aaron. Can you *really* keep a secret?"

“I can, Red, I swear!”

“All right, then.”

I step off the sidewalk and drop the card into the sewer.

27

This afternoon I cleaned all the washrooms, mopped up a puddle of vomit in Mrs. Bloom's music class and an accidental paint mess in Mr. Green's art room, collected pieces of trash on the floor, and wiped all the desks clean, among other tasks. I'm almost done mopping the floor near the administration's office. Classes ended about two hours ago, and since then everything's been quiet, like in a library. In a way I'm glad I have nothing planned with Stella later today. My legs feel like jelly, my eyelids are heavy, and I'm flat-out drained. I can't wait to go back home and pop open a beer.

Some teachers here use the walls as an art display, and every month or so the art gets replaced with new art. Other teachers like to post A-graded assignments or tests, like the one in this very hallway. I move closer to the wall. Poetry tests. All of them have colourful stickers at the top of the page, along with the word *Excellent* or *Wonderful* or *Super* and an A+ written next to them in red. I'm guessing the kids had to memorize a poem and write it all out in class. Unlike Cara, I have a poor memory. My score would've been a D, probably an F. Someone's coming out of the administration's office. It's Mayer, a fourth grader I sometimes talk to after school hours. His father's a teacher at this school.

"Hey, Mr. Red," he says, walking up to me.

"What's up, big guy? Waiting for your father?"

"Yeah. You look sleepy."

"Does it show that much?"

He nods and says, "Are you checking the poetry tests?"

"You mean these?" I glance at the wall. "Not really."

"I'm not on the wall. I never am."

"Maybe one day you will."

"I doubt it."

As soon as I go back to mopping the floor, he asks me if I like what I do.

"Very much," I tell him. "Your father's almost finished working?"

"Almost," Mayer says, and then: "My dad thinks I'll be a doctor."

"Oh, yeah?" I stop what I'm doing. "Dr. Mayer. That has a nice ring to it."

"He says that's what I should be when I grow up."

"What if you're not happy?"

"Well, he says if I'm rich, I won't struggle."

"But lots of people aren't rich and they're pretty well off. Like your teacher, Mrs. Fielding. She's happy, no?"

"I guess so. My dad wanted to be a doctor, but his grades weren't good enough. It doesn't seem like a bad job, really. When you're a doctor, you don't go to people; they come to you.

That's what my dad said."

"But what would *you* want to be? If you could be anything?"

"I'd be a comic book artist. I'd spend my time drawing all these cool superheroes. But I wouldn't be happy."

"Why's that?"

"I'd starve. My dad said there's no demand for it. He said jobs like that—like yours—don't pay, and that's not good. He doesn't want me to be like you."

"He said that?"

"Yeah. He said, 'Don't ever be like that poor janitor.' So I won't," Mayer says. "My dad—he knows these things. Maybe you should listen to him. He's a teacher after all."

IT'S A LITTLE AFTER FIVE. I go out through the main entrance, relieved and free, eager to make myself a cheeseburger and eat some ketchup chips. The air is refreshingly chilly. At first all I hear around me are the trees singing their afternoon tune, and then suddenly I hear something else: a sweet, gentle voice calling me from behind. I turn around and see her there, smiling, approaching.

"But?"

"But what?" Stella says.

"What are you doing here?"

"Just came by to say hello." She kisses me on the lips. "And to ask you if you're free, right now. You okay?"

"I'm fine. How long have you been waiting?"

"Not too long. I took a stroll around the school. You look tired, though."

"I am."

"The schoolyard's huge! I like it!"

Our faces are close. She must be wondering why my eyes keep shifting from one part of her to another. Cara's last diary entries are nothing short of unsettling. I don't know who to trust anymore, and I don't want my image of Stella to tarnish in any way. Stella's nose isn't Lacey's nose, and their mouths are like so many other mouths. Brown—that's about all they have in common. Brown eyes. Brown hair. In her diary, Cara mentions three beauty marks on Lacey's arm. Stella's hands are at her sides, so I can't see much of her arms. She looks gorgeous, so alive in that sleeveless blue dress.

"What?"

"Nothing," I say.

"Do you have anything planned? With her?"

"No."

"I was thinking of bringing you somewhere different. Like an Indian restaurant. Or maybe Mexican. But I have a craving for curry today—don't know why. So?" she says. "What do you say?"

IN THE END, HER INDIAN RESTAURANT of choice wasn't an option (temporarily closed for renovations), and there was no Mexican restaurant nearby, so we settled for Chinese. I got to eat new dishes and open a fortune cookie. (My fortune made Stella laugh: *You will meet someone very special*.) More important, I got to see *them*—the beauty marks on the front of her left arm. A straight diagonal line.

I wanted to talk to her about Lacey, to point out something they both share, but I was afraid she'd confirm Cara's suspicions; I was worried about how I'd react as a consequence, worried that my reaction would push her away, that things would never be the same, so I swept the whole matter under the rug. In any case, I don't understand why Stella would lie about her identity. Was she afraid I'd tell Cara about her? Was she afraid I wouldn't see her again?

We left the restaurant at a quarter to eight, and now I'm back home. It's eight thirty-five. I take my shoes off and walk into the living room. Papers are being flipped somewhere (in the bedroom, probably). Instead of shouting, *I'm home,* I go straight to the couch and turn on the TV. After a while, though, my head starts to loll sideways, then forward. I find myself listening to my breathing, opening my eyes only for a second or two. Then Cara emerges from our bedroom and asks me something.

"What?"

"I said do you want a beer?"

"I'll take one, thanks."

I scratch my neck and yawn as she walks up to me with two uncapped beer bottles, one in each hand. She sits down next to me, looking sombre, exhausted. Her eyes are glued to the TV screen, the beer bottles standing motionless between her thighs. For a moment I just wait for her to give me a beer, but she doesn't. I take one without asking.

"I'm guessing you had a hard day today?"

"Yeah," she answers, still staring straight ahead.

"I'll probably sleep soon."

Yawning again, I go back to watching the news. From the corner of my eye I can still see her, and I have a feeling she's scrutinizing me. An awkward tension begins to grow between us. It's making it harder for me to say something, to move a limb, even swallow. Seconds pass, but they seem like minutes. I let out a sigh, loud enough for her to hear, then turn to her. She's looking back at me, trying to read me, I think.

"What?" I ask her. "What's wrong?"

"Nothing." She repositions herself so that her back is now facing the arm of the couch. "Was it only overtime? Did you eat before coming home?"

"I did some overtime. I ate, too. I ate at McDonald's."

"Hmm…"

She moves closer to me and lays her head on my shoulder. I let my head fall on hers and wait, feeling the tension rise again.

"Do you find me prettier?"

Right away our heads part. I frown at her.

"Huh?"

"Am I prettier than her? Than that teacher, Stella?"

"Why do you ask? There's nothing going on between us—her and me."

"I know," she says, observing me. "Am I?"

Not wanting to argue or hurt her, I lie: "Yes, of course you're prettier. Why do you ask?"

"Is she nice?"

"Yeah, she's nice. But I don't understand…"

"I had a long day," she says, and gets up from the couch.

She puts her beer on the coffee table and drags her feet all the way to our bedroom. I turn the TV off and hear the bed creaking, the blanket being pulled, then nothing—nothing but the sound of my own troubled thoughts.

28

After walking two blocks in one direction, he makes a right on Richmond Street and doesn't stop until he arrives at a metro station two or three minutes later. Unlike most metro stations, this one doesn't border the sidewalk. It lies farther within the block, with paths leading up to it. Before leaving for errands, the old lady had given him directions, along with her coffee: "There's an underpass—you'll see it. The street you're looking for is somewhere on the other side."

The underpass is up ahead, but he doesn't go there just yet. He parks his grocery cart next to a water fountain and refills his plastic bottle. What with all the street and sidewalk traffic, he's guessing it's roughly noon. People are coming up from behind him, coming toward him with their ears plugged, their heads down, going in and out through the metro doors or rushing past him to catch a city bus. He realizes, as the water reaches the bottleneck, that he's not the only beggar on the same block: Along the metro wall sits a middle-aged woman with tattoos on her hands and neck—mouth partly open, brown hair dishevelled, clothes all baggy—peering at him with a zombielike expression. "I can't stay here," he says to himself, breaking eye contact. "I won't."

He screws the bottle cap and walks on with his cart, away from her prying gaze and the incessant congestion, toward the underpass. On reaching the other side, he spots a worn-out quarter on the edge of the sidewalk and picks it up eagerly. He scans the concrete floor around him but finds no other coins.

There's a bench not far away, where he can drink and think in peace. He walks up to it with his cart, the coffee cup now lukewarm to the touch, and sits down. Within minutes a mother and her child walk past him. The child, no more than four or five years of age, stops in front of the cart and lifts his hand.

"No, Mason. No! Don't touch that," his mother says.

"Look, Mom! Look!" He's pointing at something in the cart, something the beggar can't discern from the bench.

His mother then says, "Come on, Mason. Leave the man's things alone."

"It's okay," the beggar tells the boy. "Don't be afraid."

"See, Ma? He says it's okay."

But his mother takes him by the hand and pulls him away, speaking to him quietly as they walk on.

The boy, looking up, answers her shrilly, "But, Mom! Why would he be dirty?"

She whispers something to him, after which he glances at the beggar and asks, "But why would he have no home?"

The beggar watches him with the eyes of a person envious of a spoiled friend, and for a moment he pictures himself as a boy—a boy free of responsibility, of hardship and heartbreak.

When mother and son are out of sight, he puts the coffee on the ground and lies down on the bench.

His eyes don't stay open for very long. Soon after they close, all sound and movement vanish, and like magic he finds himself not lying down but sitting on the ground somewhere on Baker Street. There's a woman crouched by his side, her features ill-defined yet recognizable. He knows it's her. He stretches his hand toward his mother, his own faded image of her, and touches her cheek. Like in his previous dreams she looks calm, with no trace of sadness in her smile or disappointment in her eyes.

"Brought you something, honey. Something you like." She plunges her hands into a plastic bag lying right beside him and produces a large pie. "Your favourite," she says.

"Meat pie?"

She nods. "You must be hungry. I searched all over for you, but now I found you. Here…"

She reaches into the bag, and out comes more food: bread and chicken, an apple, a cake. She puts it all on display in front of him and gives him a fork.

"It's time to eat. Go on, honey. Eat. Are you cold?"

She sits down beside him and wraps her arm around his shoulder.

"What's wrong now?" she asks, rubbing his shoulder, ignoring the passersby before them. "What's wrong?"

The beggar runs his finger under his nose and turns to her, thinking about what to say. He feels her grip on his shoulder tighten. A faint smile starts to show on her lips.

"Ma," he says. "Ma. Will you stay with me? I have no one, Ma. I've been wandering for so long now, not doing anything, just being. But it's too late. It's too late to undo everything. I want you to know, Ma, that I think about you all the time." He pauses for a moment, sniffling, still looking at her. "I know you're not proud of me. You're disappointed, but it's okay. It's okay, Ma. I don't blame you if you are, 'cause I'm a failure after all. A waste, a nobody. Just killing time."

He's hoping to hear words of encouragement that will comfort him, prove him wrong, but he receives only silence.

"Stay," he pleads. "It would mean everything to me. You don't need to go, not again. I have a sleeping bag I can give you, I don't need it. I can buy you books. I can get them at garage sales, and you have me. You'll always have me."

He feels a knot in his throat. He feels the tears resurfacing. "Mama."

"It's all right," she says, her voice soft like the wind. "Mama."

"You'll be all right."

THE BEGGAR AWAKENS with his arm hanging like a branch over the bench. The sky hasn't changed. He figures he must have slept at most an hour. As he brings himself to a sitting position, the dream comes back to him suddenly, vividly, making his eyes burn. He finishes the coffee and walks on, past a swarm of ants feeding on an apple core, a couple unloading luggage from their car, past a man painting his front door pistachio, a woman three houses down planting flowers in her lawn, until he arrives at another main street called Orson.

Greeted by a waft of delicious scent, he cocks his head to one side and spots a businessman seated at a table on a restaurant terrace, reading a newspaper while eating grilled chicken, strips of it served with green, yellow, red vegetables all sizzling on a grill pan next to a stack of tortillas and a bowl of shredded cheese. That chicken, he tells himself, salivating. If only I could have a strip or two of that chicken. The man is so absorbed in what he's reading he has no clue two hungry eyes are watching him.

The beggar turns his cart around, away from the meal he wants to steal, and walks on. Orson Street is bustling at this hour, so he decides to stay here a while to panhandle. Unlike Baker Street, where he finds many a beggar, he sees no sign of competition on this street, in either direction.

Eventually he reaches a bank and a drugstore. He stations his cart closer to the latter, where the action is, and settles himself on the ground. A woman emerges from the drug-store with a bag hanging from her wrist. She has her wallet in one hand and some money in the other. He watches her slip a ten-dollar bill into her wallet, followed by a five-dollar bill, and only when she begins to drop in some coins does he raise his cup toward her and say, "Spare change, ma'am? Spare change, please?" The woman ignores him and walks away without uttering a word.

Then a man clad in a grey suit approaches him with coins jingling in his front pocket. "Spare change, sir?" the beggar says. "Spare change?" Without looking at him, without stop-ping, the man shakes his head and enters the drugstore.

Half an hour later the beggar's cup is still empty. Half an hour turns into an hour, and by then he's no longer sitting.

The coffee cup is on the ground now, near his face. He's using his sleeping bag as a pillow and listening, with his eyes closed, to footsteps. Waiting patiently, as he always does, for the clink of metal.

29

Cara left not long ago. She's having brunch with friends. "I don't know when I'll be back. Don't wait for me," she said, on her way out. It's now ten fifteen. Apart from doing the laundry, I have no other chore scheduled for today. I'm tempted to go back to bed and sleep a little longer, but there's something else I'd like to do first. Something I certainly can't do when Cara's home.

It's strange, though. As much as I find her diary entries bruising, I can't get enough of them; I can't stop thinking about all of those entries still waiting to be read. I'd rather know her thoughts, her own truths, than make assumptions about them. I'd rather be bruised.

I open the closet in our room and remove the lid from one of Cara's blue plastic containers. All four diaries are still there, in one neat stack just like I left them. I settle myself on the living room couch with one diary on my lap and the other three beside me. As I stare at the words *My Life* written in her own hand on the cover, two crossed-out sentences from my previous readings come back to haunt me: *I hope you live a terrible life* and *You don't deserve a happy ending.* I don't blame her for hating me, but I don't deserve to be unhappy. That's not something I'd ever wish on anyone.

I open the diary. The first page is a pencil drawing of a bridge with grassy mounds around it, and two happy-faced stick figures. My name is under one of them. Below my name, alone near the bottom of the page, is the word *Emerald* in green. I turn the page, and now all I see are words, tiny magnets drawing me to them. *Emerald is the name of my park,* she wrote on the very first line. And then:

> *I like it. I asked dad once what it meant and*
> *he said it is a stone. A green stone. There's a lot*
> *of green in my park but no green stone, so the*
> *name is not fitting well with the park. But the*
> *name is pretty. Of all names Micky is the best*
> *name in our park, even better than mine. I don't*
> *like him but I still talk to him yesterday outside*
> *in the night with everybody around. He said*
> *Red and him go to the store later to buy candy.*
> *When I asked him about Red he did not say so*
> *much. I always think he keeps things to himself*
> *like secrets because he looks down or somewhere*
> *away from my eyes. He is loyol which is good,*
> *but he looks like a nerd. Once I asked him who*
> *he likes best and he said Red. I asked him why*
> *and he said he just was and that they known*
> *each other since they were little, and because Red*

*is nice to him and cares about him and he likes
being with Red. That is a very good answer.
Nobody ever said that about me though. Maybe
one day someone will.*

Flipping a few pages, I come across an entry with heart stickers here and there in the margin. By chance I spot my name somewhere in one paragraph, and again on the very first line.

*I think Red likes me. Today we were on the
bridge all together except Hank and Finne. And
I realize Red sometimes checks me out when we
are not speaking. Twice I saw him look at me
while I was with Lacey, he looked at me only.
He did not smile but it does not matter. Even
Lacey said he checks me out when I was at her
house. She told me Red might have a crush
on me. I asked her why. She said because I'm
prettier than her and taller, and also smarter. I
decided to put heart stickers on this page because
it's love ♥.*

*I think about Red a lot and I love him. Maybe
he's my boyfriend. He's a boy after all, and he's
my friend. But he would also be Lacey's boyfriend to, so I guess that doesn't work. There is
no boy I have a crush at school. Red is the only
boy I love and he's not at my school. His face is
very nice, an angel face. And his eyes are big and
bright. Not long ago I dreamed that we were in*

*my school play ground and I was showing him
to my friends like my favourite toy. And we
were holding hands like a real growup couple.
It was a good dream because I felt happy in it.
I was sad to leave it. Maybe I should tell him
my feelings. But I am afraid he will react bad
and tell me something I don't wanna hear or
that makes me sad and then I will regret telling
him in the first place. It should be him to tell
me about his feelings first because he is the boy.
Maybe he is shy that's all.*

*Anyway I feel in a good mood and I hope that
he will show up in the park tomorrow. That
way I can spend time with him alone. Even if
they are there it does not matter that much. If
we play kick the can I will try to hide with him
if he is not it. He'll try to follow Lacey, but I
will follow him. I hope Lacey won't be there. I
always hope that when he's around.*

The next entry isn't written the same way. Each letter of our names occupies a separate line, and written beside these letters is a message. A small pink heart, alone on one line, links our names together.

Red *is his name but it is also a colour. It's not his
favourite colour I think. My favourite colour is
yellow like the sun*

*Extraordinary. I looked it up in the dictionnary.
It means to be exceptional and very unsual.
Maybe Red is both*

*Dreamy. It took me a long time to find some
word with D that makes me think of Red. But
sometimes he makes me have a dream of him so
that's why he's dreamy. I wonder if I'm in his
dreams ever? I will ask Lacey because maybe she
knows. I will ask her tomorrow.*

♥

*Chocolate is my favourite desert. It's too bad I
don't get to much of it because my parents don't
want to buy any. They say it's bad for my health.
I don't like when they say that*

*Astronaut is what I wanna be when I grow
up. To do that I will need to study space science.
It seems like a complicated subjeck but I will be
ready obviously. And I am smart also.*

*Red is the man I wanna marry. I hope we get
four children. Two boys and two girls. I'd call
the girls Sally and Ella, and the boys Charlie
and Danny*

*Amphibian. It is a word I learned in English
class this year. It's an ugly word if you ask me*

> *and I don't like frogs. I did not want to put*
> *amphibian but I couldn't find any word that*
> *starts with the letter A except for And and All.*
> *Now I found one, it's the word Amazing. But*
> *it's too late. I can't erase everything I wrote*
> *above because it took awhile to write it all and*
> *it is just too late*

Unable to wait any longer, I close the diary and open the one with the black cover. I feel like I've eaten only appetizers up to this point. The main course is now on my lap. Anxiously I flip the pages until I get to the last of her entries, which I still haven't read. I certainly don't expect it to be funny or enjoyable like some of her previous ones. I'm scared to read it, but I can't wait any longer.

> *I thought it was nothing at all. I thought I had*
> *it all wrong, but now that I <u>know</u> I can't take*
> *it anymore. I can't. For the past hour I've been*
> *obsessing about where he is, what he's doing, and*
> *it's driving me insane. We haven't been talkative*
> *lately, and we're barely in the same room together*
> *when we're not asleep. But this afternoon I*
> *wanted to break the ice. I thought maybe I'd pay*
> *him a surprise visit—I'd pick him up at work*
> *and we'd eat out somewhere and talk.*

> *Sticking to my plan I drove to his school, but*
> *when I got there I saw that bitch Stella ambling*
> *about near the entrance door. I found a parking*

space farther along the block and went for it, thinking I'd chat with her for a while before the end of Red's shift. That didn't happen. She wasn't ambling about for the fun of it. She was waiting for him to come out! And when he did she went up to him and kissed him. And he kissed her back. He kissed her! I just sat there in my car, powerless, overwhelmed, angry and shocked, jealous, devastated all at once. He seemed happy. What does she give you that makes you so happy? This so-called Stella? This bitch who's obviously not who she says she is? I knew there was something familiar about her, but gullible Cara brushed it off. I needed to know the truth so I finally visited my parents and went through a few old albums. I found what I was looking for: pictures of Lacey posing with me, sitting on the bridge, standing by my side in my parents' backyard.

There's no denying it: Stella is Lacey. But you probably know this already, don't you? Want to see her? Go to the very last page. Yes, I'm addressing you, Red. You think I don't know you've been reading my diaries? You think I'd never find out about your affair? You disgust me. You had no right to read my diaries. How dare you? How could you do something like that? You had <u>no right</u>.

Your silence—our silence needs to stop. How long can we go on without talking to each other about the affair? About us? How long, Red, before it's too late?

I turn to the very last page. The picture she's referring to is glued to the inside back cover with a piece of Scotch tape. There's my Lacey, smiling at me on the bridge, with Cara by her side. For some time I find myself studying those lovely features I once knew so well, more than my own, all the while picturing Stella, comparing her to Lacey, wanting them to be the same person and yet not wanting them to. I close the diary and put all four of them away, thinking long and hard about Stella.

30

Mickey's room is very different from my own. We both have a bed, a desk to do our homework, and a drawer chest, but Mickey has things I don't have and more of the things I have. More figurines and other toys. More books. More board games. I'm playing with some of his soldier figurines and race cars at the foot of his bed. He's sitting next to me, putting together a railroad set his parents bought for him earlier today. There's also a train ten cars long that goes with it. Since I got here we've talked from time to time but not much each time. I put the toys down and look at his tree-brown eyes, at his glasses that make his eyes look bigger than they are, and I ask him if they all hate me.

"Who hates you?" Mickey says.

"Everyone in the park."

"Not everyone. Not me."

"I wasn't counting you, Mickey. I know we'll always be friends. But Hank and Finn..."

"Who cares about them?"

"I don't know why they hate me so much. I never did nothing."

"They pick on people, that's why. They're bullies."

"Rex has something against me. Like I did something bad to him."

"He wants to be Hank. He'll do whatever Hank tells him just to fit in and be liked. He doesn't know what he's doing, that's what."

"They know I'm poor."

"So?"

"I'm not like them."

Mickey doesn't answer. He's attaching the chimney to the train.

"Lacey. Does she like me?"

"She never said she did, not to me."

"But do you think she does?"

"Maybe. I mean, you're always together."

"That's not true."

"A lot, then. Outside anyhow. Last time no one knew where you guys were. We had to start the game all over. I went to the other side of the bridge, thinking you were hiding there. I was trying to find you."

"I should've told you, Mickey."

"I hid in the farthest alleyway. Hank never found me. He had to go eat after you kicked the ball. When I got to the other block, you weren't there. Where did you go?"

"Home. I didn't want to stay. But I should've told you. I didn't want to play it their way, always me being the seeker, always me. I'm sick of being the seeker, Mickey. I'm sick of them cheating all the time."

"Last time you lost the rock-paper-scissors match, fair and square."

"No, Mickey. Hank and Finn *chose* us to go head-to-head. They always choose. What about us? Why can't we choose? And if it's not rock-paper-scissors, then they force me to be it. They force me. So last time I fought back, Mickey, and I don't regret it. I'm glad Hank was it, and I'm glad I kicked that damn ball."

Mickey's almost done putting his railroad set together. He's placing little houses along the tracks. I turn my attention back to the race cars beside me. Among them I pick up a green one with a smiling skull on its hood and big red flames on its doors. I start spinning one of the wheels with my finger, thinking about what I want for my birthday.

"I know you like her," Mickey says, setting the train on the tracks. He looks up at me, waiting for an answer. He's waiting for me to spill the beans.

I stare at the race car, but after a while I can tell, even with my head down, that his eyes are still on me.

Finally he says, "I've seen you, Red. I've seen you spying on her a lot, but that's okay. I've already done the same thing before and other boys, too. There's this girl I like at my school. Her name's Bridgitte."

"Really?"

He nods.

"I guess I…I like her, yeah."

"I'm pretty sure she does, too, now that I think of it. Sometimes I hear them talk about boys and stuff."

"Lacey and Cara?"

"Yeah. It's a girl thing," he says. "That's all girls talk about."

I get up and go to the window, which looks out onto the park. I step onto his wooden chair for a better view. The flowers in Mickey's backyard seem a bit different from where I'm standing. Along the fence are violet flowers shaped like popsicles, yellow flowers with bushy heads, pink ones between them, but I don't know any of their names. Near the balcony stairs sits the barbecue, covered from head to toe in a black cloak. The backyard table is in the middle, with six chairs around it. The only thing unpretty is the fence on the right-hand side, which isn't a straight line. As usual there's Mickey's neighbour to the left, smoking a cigar at his table, relaxing in a chair with his feet resting on the seat of another chair. Farther out I see parasols sticking out above backyard fences, empty chairs on balcony floors, pots of flowers hanging from balcony rails, and now there she is, far away from me but not too far, opening her balcony door. She doesn't know I'm watching her take the stairs. When she opens her backyard door, I say, "Mickey…Mickey I'm gonna go outside."

"Why?"

"Just want to. It's okay if you stay here. You should play with your railroad set."

"You sure?"

"Yeah."

"Okay," he says. "I'll see you later."

Lacey's still there when I enter the park. She sees me coming and waves. I give myself a push, and now I'm running, feeling like a boat somewhere far away, in an ocean. For a moment the park looks so different, not like a real park: The squirrels have turned into fish with fluffy tails, the bushes into sea creatures from another world; the mounds are no longer mounds but waves, all still and bright green. Without stopping I head straight for the bridge, the brown desert island where she is.

"What's up, Lacey?" I'm on the island, taking a seat opposite her on the rail.

"Nothing. Just playing with my Slinky," she says, stretching and shortening her pink toy like an accordion. "What did you do today?"

"I was with Mickey. Other than that, not much. What about you?"

"I went shopping with my parents. And this afternoon I drew a little bit."

"What did you draw?"

"Mermaids. And flowers."

"That's cool… Lacey?"

"What?"

"Sorry about the other day."

"It wasn't your fault."

"Your mother must've been angry."

"No, it's fine."

"You sure?"

"Yeah."

"'Cause Cara sounded like your mother was worried."

"Cara wasn't happy 'cause we were over there and she was over here by herself," she says, twirling her hair. "Cara gets jealous pretty easily."

"Did you tell her about it?"

"The kiss? No."

She gets up, crosses the deck of the bridge, and takes a seat next to me on the rail.

"So did you like it?" I ask her.

She smiles, making me smile, and starts giggling.

"What?" I ask.

"Nothing. You want to try again?"

"Do you?"

"I don't mind."

She's waiting for me to make a move. I can't stop staring at her eyes, her lips, her eyes, her lips. I lean in, and she closes her eyes. The kiss doesn't last long, maybe two or three seconds, tops. We get up and start walking on the path. She's holding the Slinky with her right hand, so I take her left hand in my right. She doesn't shake it away, but she looks at me a bit surprised, a bit happy. We cut through the grass and keep walking, hand in hand like a real couple, until I spot Rex heading down the balcony stairs. I let go of her hand, and then Rex opens his backyard door. Running up to us, he sings, "Red and Lacey sitting in the tree...*K-I-S-S-I-N-G*. First comes love...then comes marriage...then comes the baby in the baby carriage!"

"What are you talking about?" I ask.

"You love each other. Admit it!"

"Shut up, Rex. You don't know what you're saying."

"I saw you from my room window! I saw you two kissing on the bridge. Don't lie!"

Does Lacey want me to lie? I can't read her, and I can't ask her in front of this asshole.

"It's not what you think, Rex," Lacey says.

"You kissed. Just admit it."

Cara opens her backyard door. She runs up to us and asks, "Hey, what's going on?"

Rex tells her what he saw us do. Cara doesn't answer, but her eyes and mouth tell me she's shocked, in a bad way. She turns to Lacey, who looks back at her, then at me, as if she's waiting for me to say something. I'm blushing, I know it; I'm starting to get nervous 'cause there's a chance Rex will blab about the whole thing to everybody. He probably will.

"Did you kiss him, Lacey?" Cara asks. "Did he kiss you?"

Twirling her hair, Lacey doesn't say anything.

"It just happened," I finally answer.

"So it *did* happen," Cara says.

Rex doesn't keep quiet. "I was right! I was right all along! You can't fool me, Red!"

"Why did you kiss her," Cara says, "if you don't even like her?"

"I never said that, Cara. Don't put words in my mouth. I never said that, ever."

"Well, do you?"

"I… It's none of your business."

"Well, she doesn't like you."

"Yeah, she does."

"Maybe as a friend, but not that way. Right?" she says, looking at Lacey.

I can tell Lacey's not enjoying this conversation at all. I'm not, either. Everything was going just fine until Rex and Cara came along and spoiled it. Lacey steps away from us. She's heading toward Cara's house, but why? We watch her go away, and then I see them; I see those pink and yellow chalks lying on the path near Cara's backyard. Crouching, Lacey puts her Slinky on the ground and picks up a chalk. Even from here I can tell she's drawing hopscotch squares on the path. Cara leaves us to join her.

"So what do you want to do?" Rex asks me.

"Huh?"

"What do you want to play?"

We decide to play a bit of Frisbee. Rex goes back home to get his Frisbee while I watch their mouths move. Cara's doing most of the talking, Lacey most of the listening. Cara keeps looking back and forth at me and Lacey. I catch Lacey looking at me but only for a second.

I wonder what Cara's telling her.

31

I'm with Stella, in her car. Earlier this morning she picked me up at a café three blocks away from my apartment, looking real nice with her black sunglasses and glossy pink lipstick. We've been in the car for about an hour, listening to a bit of blues, a bit of jazz, not talking much. Instead of staring at the road ahead, I'm watching the trees flitter past me beyond the open window, all the while thinking about Cara's last diary entry.

Since reading it I've been keeping my distance from her, reflecting more on everything, speaking less. At home I'm finding it harder to look at Cara in the eye, to fall asleep with her lying so close to me. But what if she's right? What if Stella really *is* Lacey after all? At first I was afraid to know, afraid to ask, but now I want to know, I want the truth. I've been checking out her profile on and off from my side of the car. I see a resemblance. I see it more now.

Stella glances at me. "What?" she asks.

"Nothing." I turn away, still thinking.

Within minutes the car slows down, and Stella says we're almost there. She won't tell me where we're going, but I find out soon enough when we pass a green sign with the word *beach* in white. It doesn't take long before the sand and the slanted parasols come into view. For a moment I look down at my sweaty palms, at my left leg shaking on its own.

"Surprise!"

I give her a quick smile. She notices my unease as we enter the parking lot.

"What's wrong?" she asks.

"Nothing."

"Are you sure?"

"Yeah. I'm fine."

"I thought maybe we'd do something completely different. Away from the city."

I expected the surprise to be less different. Like lunch at a new restaurant, or even bowling.

The beach we're at has a forest on both sides. We head for the one on the left, which happens to be lying on a bed of rock overlooking the water. Sitting unoccupied among the trees are two picnic tables, both shaded and streaked with light. As we make our way to the farthest of the two, my mind gets distracted by the lake and the people bobbing in it, by the bodies lying face up or face down on the sand, and soon my hands start to sweat again.

After putting Stella's bag of beach essentials on the table, I walk up to the forest's edge where the rock below meets the water, and there I gaze at the waves approaching, getting bigger, crashing into the rock. Stella comes up to me with our lunch, and we decide to eat right there, on the forest's edge.

We take a seat on the rocky floor, our feet dangling, almost touching the water.

I'll make a sand castle, I tell myself, sipping through a straw. If not a castle, then a turtle. Maybe a heart or *S+R*. The food is excellent (chicken ranch wraps with barbecue chips and cheese cubes), the weather perfect for a beach day. Stella's speaking between mouthfuls about what she plans on doing once she goes back to New York. I'd rather she change the subject. Despite my attempts at convincing her to stay, she won't. I thought about going with her, leaving everything I know behind. Problem is, I don't know what's out there. I can't see how I could ever be happy elsewhere, jobwise and all. The other day I told her I love her, which is true. I tell her, "I love you," just now. She touches my cheek.

"Don't be sad," she says.

"But I am, Stella. I am."

"Don't be."

"Then don't leave."

I watch her gaze shift from my eyes to the water, her hair waving gently in the wind. She has a calmness about her that Cara doesn't have; it's as if she knows everything will be all right somehow, for the both of us. She says she hasn't been to this lake in the longest time, but her memories of it are happy ones.

"There's something about this place—the sound of the waves, or being in the water—that would make everything go away for a time. All the stress. Any bad thought," she says. "Just for a time."

After a short pause she turns to me. Her eyes are troubled. "Red..."

I wait for the rest, but she doesn't say it. "What is it? What's wrong?"

She looks away, but I don't. I want the truth.

"Is it about you? Or did I do something wrong?" I ask.

"No." She shakes her head. "It's—"

We both start to speak at the same time.

"Go ahead," I tell her.

"It's just… I miss being here. I miss the sounds."

"You miss the sounds."

"Yeah… Why don't we go for a swim? Not now but later."

I don't answer.

"After my fruit salad?"

"You can go. I'll watch you. I don't have a bathing suit anyway."

"You can go in with your shorts."

"Yeah, but…they're not like a bathing suit."

"Oh, I think so."

"I don't know…"

"Red?" she says, waiting for an answer. "What's wrong?"

"It's nothing. I've never been much of a swimmer."

"You know how to swim, don't you?"

I hold her stare, but I don't shake my head. She knows, I think. She knows, and so I look down.

"It's all right," she says. "I can show you how. We don't need to stay long."

"I don't know, Stella."

"I'll be with you," she says with a note of calmness, of re-assurance. "But it's all right if you don't. I don't want to force you or anything."

"It's okay. I know you don't." Still, I tell myself, glancing at the lake, at the shimmering waves, still I should go with her. I should try at least.

"I'll go with you," I tell her. "I want to."

"You sure?"

I hear splashing. Bursts of laughter. With an inward smile I say, "Yeah, Stella, I'm sure. Let's do it."

LATER, AFTER A BRIEF HIKE in the forest and some dessert (a fruit salad for Stella and a chocolate bar for me), we find ourselves walking in the water. We're sinking together, sinking slowly, holding each other by the hand. We stop when the water line reaches our shoulders. Witnessing the insecurity on my face, Stella tightens her grip and says, "It's all right."

"It's…it's not so bad."

"Let the waves push you. When the next wave comes, jump a little," she says, and lets go of my hand.

The next wave appears. Before it reaches me, I jump a little; I surrender to it. My heart skips a beat as we embrace, as it pushes me softly.

"Try it again," she says.

And so I do. Wave after wave I lift my feet and move backward, feeling exhilarated and free. Stella laughs, and I tell her I like it; now she's saying something too quickly, something I can't make out.

"What's that?"

"I can pick you up," she shouts.

"In the water?"

"In the water."

I don't believe her, but she insists she can, so I let her try. We step back until the water line stops near our belly buttons.

"Put your arm around my neck," she says, and reaches for my legs. "It's okay. Let your legs go. I have you."

I let my legs go, and the next thing I know I'm in her arms, bobbing on the waves.

"That's amazing!"

"Not really," she says. "The water's doing all the work for me."

"It's still amazing."

She brings me back to a standing position. "Do you want to go back? Or we can stay."

"No."

"No?"

"I want to stay. Just a little longer."

We go a bit deeper into the water, and she says, "I'm going to hold you while you tread."

"What's that?"

"You'll see. Let yourself go."

Anxious yet uncertain, I let myself go. She lifts my legs with one arm while holding my midsection with the other. Now I'm like a log floating in the water. I feel unstable, though, and there's a wave approaching. She tells me to bring my hands up before me and paw.

"Like a dog," she says.

I start pawing, and then a wave hits me on the side of my face. My hands freeze. I gasp and say, "I don't know. I can't. I can't."

"I'm holding you. I'm here, keep pawing." Her voice is calm, encouraging. I start pawing again, and she says, "That's it. Keep pawing. You can move your legs up and down, up and down. I'm holding you."

The next wave comes, but this time nothing bad happens and so I go on pawing and kicking, listening to the water, to Stella's voice among the waves.

"There you go… That's it."

"I—I can do it. I can swim."

"Keep pawing. I'm not leaving."

"I really like it, Stella."

"I knew you would. You're doing great… That's it. I have you, Red."

"Stella."

"I have you."

32

When he opens his eyes, the coffee cup isn't where it should be. Instead of being upright near his face, it's lying on its side by the wheel of a parked car. The wind, he thinks, must have pushed it there. He rises to his feet, yawning, and rubs his eyes. The sun is elsewhere, the daylight weakening. Before he continues his quest, he retrieves his coffee cup—still empty, to his dismay—and puts it back into his cart. He moves on, past more stores and restaurants, past an art gallery, a gas station, until he reaches the next intersection. There he makes a right and crosses. Walking now on Nelson Street, the beggar enters a residential area marked with yellow speed limit signs.

His former elementary school is up ahead, on the corner of the next block. He recognizes its brick colour, a serene orange visible between the trees. Just the sight of it makes him think of the old lady on the bench and parts of their conversation.

In less than a minute he steps onto the block. He leaves his cart under a tree and walks up to the green chain-link fence surrounding the school. Leaning against the fence, his fingers wrapped around the wires, he marvels at the children's artwork plastered on the windows, the chalk drawings strewn over the playground floor. Fond memories of this place begin to surface. Memories of Valentine chocolates and Easter candy bags; lunch-hour ball games, races, and tag; his music teacher, Miss Betsy, and her sleek trombone; the blackboards, the classrooms, his bus rides home.

Feeling a sense of calm lightheartedness, he returns to his cart and resumes his walk down Nelson Street, still thinking, until he stops next to a public trash can. Unmindful of onlookers, he plunges his hands into the rubbish, shifting an empty juice box, crumpled wrappings, and chewed-up fruits but finds nothing worth taking—nothing save a zip-lock bag of smoked almonds. He opens the bag and counts twenty almonds, two of which he pops into his mouth. He reaches into the bag for more and takes out three, keeping the rest for another time, and walks on.

When he arrives at the next intersection, he stops and looks around. Dead ahead, under a pinkish sky, stands the local church with its Gothic windows, its crooked hatlike spire. While over there, across the street to his left, are low-rise apartment buildings as far as the eye can see, backed by the white glow of the sky above the rooftops, a white that segues into vaporous blue higher up and beyond.

The beggar turns left toward the apartments and the white-blue sky, feeling the need to urinate. He passes the first apartment building, then the second, listening as he goes to voices, cutlery noises, and shouts echoing through open doors and windows. One voice in particular, more distinct than the rest, addresses him from behind. Turning around he sees no one, but then a hand starts waving at him from a window on the second floor of a three-storey apartment building, the one he's just passed. "Come," says the old man in a gentle, raspy voice. Suddenly he disappears from the window.

The beggar pulls his cart backward, perplexed. The old man opens a sliding door and steps onto his balcony, carrying a cardboard box. He places it on the handrail, steadying it between his hands, and gazes down at that face, a picture of pity and languor, at those brown unblinking eyes gazing up at him.

"I was wondering," he says, "if you'd like a few things. It's not much, though."

"Anything you're willing to give, sir, I'll take."

The old man reaches into the box and produces a grey sweater. "There's also some food in here. Some Lipton soup packs, a sack of oatmeal and raisin boxes, a few other things. If you want, you can have this sweater. It doesn't fit me anymore, but I hardly ever wore it anyway. I'd say it looks almost brand new! Truth is, I was planning on giving some boxes to the Salvation Army and some to the church, but I don't mind if you take this one."

"I'll take it. I'll take anything," the beggar says, thinking about all the free food he'll be getting, the soup packs in particular.

"Good!" the old man says. "You in a hurry?"

"No, just strolling. It's a fine day to do that."

"Sure is." He squints at the sky. "My wife's favourite hobby."

"What is, sir?"

"Strolling. Our morning ritual, after breakfast. We never got tired of it, though."

"I walk about an hour a day. It's good for your bones."

"Oh, I agree."

"I do most of my daily strolling downtown. It's the place I know best."

"Orson for us," the old man says. "That was our spot. We'd go all the way there and stop at that French café. What's the name again…?"

"I wouldn't know, sir."

"Chez Murielle—yes, that's it. We'd have tea at Chez Murielle by the window, a croissant every now and then. Of course when my wife died, I stopped going. I had no reason to keep going 'cause it was our thing," he says. "If one of us goes, then it's no longer ours, is it? But I'm grateful it was." After a short pause he adds, as if talking to himself, "Maybe I should take a stroll, not now but some other time, or walk to Orson for a cup of tea—maybe a croissant, what the heck! Tomorrow. I think I'll go there tomorrow, just for us."

"Sounds like a great idea to me."

"You think so?"

"If I were you, I'd do it."

For a moment the old man looks away, indecisive, pondering. "Oh, why the hell not?!" he exclaims.

Picking up the box, the old man walks back inside, leaving the beggar speechless and confused. After a while he begins to fear the worst: that the old man had a sudden change of heart. Was it something I said? he asks himself. Was I insulting? Crestfallen, frustrated at himself, the beggar pushes his cart and walks on, not wanting to. He doesn't go far. At the sound of a shout, he stops abruptly and glances over his shoulder. The old man is making his way to him, holding not one but two boxes, the top one arriving just above his chin. The beggar turns around to face him.

"Sorry for the delay," the old man says. "I thought maybe you'd want more food." He hands him both boxes. "I'll leave you to your strolling, then."

He's about to leave when the beggar tells him to wait.

"Is there something you want me to do?"

"No. Please wait." The beggar, choked with emotion, puts the boxes on the ground by his cart and starts rummaging through his things. As soon as he finds what he's looking for, he brings it to him.

The old man takes the keychain—a tiny, sparkly blue soccer ball—and examines it under the fading light. "It's nice," he says, turning it in his hand. "Quite nice. But I think you should keep it."

"I want you to have it, sir."

The old man hesitates.

"I got it as a gift," the beggar says. "I know it's not much. It's just an old keychain, but it's the best piece of me and you should have it. I'll be real happy if you take it."

"Well, if that's what you want."

"It is."

The old man turns the keychain in his hand one more time. "All right," he says. "All right, I'll keep it."

Heading back to his apartment building, the old man stops about midway and wheels around. "By the way," he shouts, watching the beggar turn toward him, "I threw in some chocolate chip cookies for you. I hope you like them. Made them myself!"

THE BEGGAR, PUSHING HIS CART with renewed vigour, can't wait to sit down and peruse the contents of both boxes. Since parting with the old man a few minutes ago, he's been debating whether he should take a break or find a place to urinate. But the thought of biting into a homemade cookie—soft inside, crispy at the top, with big chocolate chunks—gets the better of him. Without waiting any longer, he stops next to an apartment building fronted by a small stretch of lawn. Between the sidewalk and the lawn stands a knee-high rail, somewhat jagged, its black paint chipped in certain places. He takes a seat on the rail with the boxes heaped on his lap and looks around for prying eyes. Finding none, he sets the boxes on the ground beside him and puts the top one on his lap and opens it.

The sweater greets him first. He stretches it out like a bedsheet and examines the knitting pattern, the sleeves, before placing it over the rail. He can see some of his other presents, all neatly arranged: a pocketbook, a deck of cards, two mugs, three pairs of black socks, a cereal box, peanut butter, and blueberry jam, not to mention some underwear.

He puts the box down and picks up the other one, which, according to the old man, has more food in it. "Good Lord," he whispers, on opening the flaps. His hand reaches for the ziplock bag of cookies and brings one up to his mouth. He's not at all disappointed. After gobbling it up in two bites, he grabs another one and starts eating it slowly as he takes out, inspects, puts back in a bag of chips, apple sauce containers, a box of oats. Just a few scoops of those oats, he tells himself, taking one last bite of the cookie—just a few will keep my stomach full for a while. Now his eyes are fixated on the bag of sliced bread and the tangerines clustered together in one corner.

Never before has he felt so elated. Giving away the keychain was the least I could do, he thinks, and wanting to do so was genuine. But now, as he pictures it before his eyes, sparkling like crystal, as he reminisces about that day, that moment when he first had it in his hand, now he wants to see it, to hold it again under the light, just for a second.

He misses it already.

33

Today is a terrible day. Not because of where we are or what we're doing, or because of anything she said to me or I to her. It's terrible because Stella's leaving. Her flight is scheduled for eleven a.m. tomorrow. I wanted today to be special for her, so we had supper at a vintage French restaurant downtown. Our final stop is out here, at a drive-in.

The field is about half occupied. We're more or less in the centre of it all, chilling on my beach towel by the wheel of Stella's car. I'm sitting cross-legged while Stella has her arms wrapped around her knees and her head leaning against my shoulder. Two plastic cups, each filled with red wine, stand upright on the grass near the edge of my beach towel. Suspended above us, above everything, is a blueish star-spangled darkness. And floating in rippled sheets across this darkness are the clouds, sombre-looking but thin enough so that you can see through them. Below the sky, behind the movie screen, lies a forest so dense, so dark I can't make out a single trunk or leaf on any tree. It really is a background of pure black, darker than any blacks in the sky.

The featured film is called *Casablanca*. It's an old black-and-white film, and I don't recognize any of the actors. I'm not sure what's going on because my mind is elsewhere, far away from this place. I'm thinking about tomorrow and about after tomorrow, when everything will go back to the way it was. I put my hand on her shoulder and watch her eyes move, wondering whether she's watching and listening or watching and thinking. She tilts her head up and smiles. I feel my lips starting to curl, but I don't smile back. She straightens herself, her head no longer resting on my shoulder, and thanks me for the supper, the movie, and the wine. Just by looking at me she knows something's on my mind.

"What is it?"

I start tugging at the grass near my shoe, and my eyes are getting sleepy.

"Tell me," she insists.

"You already know." I feel a knot in my throat. "It was worth it, all of it. Everything we did. And I meant everything I said to you, about you."

I pull out of my pocket a small blue box. "For you."

Her eyes widen. "For me?"

I put the box in her hands. She brings it up to her ear and shakes it delicately. We hear something jingle inside.

"Jewelry," she says.

She opens the box and looks up at me, surprised, her mouth opening, and takes out the ankle bracelet. I watch her fingers run over the star pendants.

"It's gorgeous, Red. It really is. But it's too much."

I smile.

"You didn't have to."

"Stella, it's yours. Here, show me your foot."

I take the bracelet and put it around her ankle and fasten it for her. The star pendants are glowing like her eyes, like tiny light bulbs.

"I wanted you to have something nice, something that will remind you of me when you wear it."

She's looking down, her fingers interacting with the stars. "That's really sweet of you. But I just… I didn't get you anything."

"Well, that's not very fair, is it?"

She laughs and tells me she has something to compensate for the missing gift.

"The thing is that lately I've…I've been thinking a lot about everything, what I want, about us, too. It's going to be hard at first—"

"Are you…? No. No, it can't be. You're leaving."

"I'm gonna stay. I've decided to stay."

"What?"

She nods. Her eyes are still glowing, but my spirit is glowing even more than her eyes, the movie screen, the stars combined. I lean in and we kiss. We embrace.

"I have to settle things in New York. I still have to go back."

"That's fine."

"I'll have to apply for a job here."

"That's fine, too."

She lets go of me. "Red?"

"Yeah?"

"There's something else. But you won't like it."

I don't say anything. I don't look away.

"I lied to you."

"Stella."

"I lied. I'm so sorry, Red."

I draw her toward me, letting her head fall on my shoulder. "I know."

"What?" she asks, straightening herself.

"I know what you're going to say."

"You do?"

"Cara recognized you. I found out from her."

"Red."

"You're Lacey. You're my Lacey."

"I am," she says, smiling like someone who's about to cry.

"Why?" I ask. "Why pretend you're someone else?"

"I wanted to tell you, Red. I tried to."

As much as I want to say something, I don't. There's a silence between us, a silence that shouldn't be here.

"The bar," she says. "When you told me her name at the bar, I knew. I knew at that moment who you both were. I remembered just how much she liked you, how jealous she was back then. It was like the past was now the present, but I didn't want that. I didn't want her to know I was even talking to you. I didn't want to get in the way."

"But you *did* get in the way. And I'm glad, Lacey."

"It was Stella who did, not your Lacey from Emerald Park, if that makes any sense."

"I don't know. I don't know what to think, really."

"I shouldn't have lied. I shouldn't have."

I wipe away the tear on her cheek. "Everything will be all right." Is that all, though? Is there more to the truth? Did she think I'd reject her? Did she?

"Red."

"It's all right."

Of course it's not all right. I have every reason to be furious, to feel betrayed. I have every reason to take back everything I said about her that was good, to end our relationship. But when I think about the lies I've told Cara, about the things I've done behind her back, I can't say I'm any better. Truth is, I'm much worse.

"What's done is done. We can't change it."

"I feel terrible, Red. It was wrong, and I'm—"

"I know. It's okay."

"Do you forgive me?"

After a short pause I tell her, "I do. Of course I do."

"I'm so sorry."

"I know, Lacey." I put my hand on her shoulder. "What's done is done."

It's late when I arrive home. I'm walking slowly, trying to be as light on my feet as possible. The darkness around me has streaks of outdoor light in it, so I can still see where I'm going. I pass by our room (Cara's in bed, fast asleep) as I make my way to the kitchen. I take out the pitcher from the fridge, pour myself a glass of fruit punch, and now, between sips, I look around at the furniture and television set, the pictures and copycat paintings on the walls, the papers lying on the table, and wonder what life will be like once I leave this place, this home I've known for the past two years, and move in with Stella—I mean, with Lacey.

I tiptoe into our room and remove my clothes. Cara's lying on her side facing me, stirring a little as I slide into bed. It doesn't take long before I start picturing scenes of us that may…that *will* probably happen following my confession: scenes of her shouting at me, venting her anger, storming out of the apartment crying. As soon as I turn my head toward her, my body freezes. She's awake. Staring at me with dark, almost frightening eyes. I say nothing, but I don't look away, I don't move an inch. Suddenly, her eyes close.

34

The buzzer rings. I run out of my room and press the button on the wall to let her in. I hope she doesn't mind lemon pie as an afternoon snack. If I had money, I'd buy my friends doughnuts and chocolate bars, all kinds of jujubes—anything to make them stay. To make them happy. Isn't that what friends would do? I open the door, and within seconds Lacey shows up with a plastic container between her hands. She has a pink barrette shaped like a flower on the side of her head, and her eyes are shiny, like glass.

I close the door behind her. "Mickey's already here."

"Okay." She holds out the container. "I brought you this," she says, and puts it in my hands. The container is see-through, so I know what's inside.

"Thanks, Lacey. They look real good."

She follows me to the kitchen. I open the cupboard and take out two plates.

"I have some lemon pie if you want."

"Yeah, I'll take some," she says, acting a little shy. "Is your mom home?"

"No. But she'll be back soon."

I place a spoon on each plate, then cut two pieces of lemon pie, one for Lacey and one for Mickey. I give Lacey her plate and she says, "You're not eating some pie?"

"I'd rather eat your cupcakes."

"My mom made them today, with my help."

"I'm sure I'll like them. My ma didn't make the pie, though." I'm walking with Mickey's dessert in one hand and a cupcake in the other. The spoon is sliding across the plate, the bottom part of it already buried in lemon slush. "She bought it at the grocery store."

"My mom told me that homemade food is better than any other food."

"I didn't know that. Ma's food isn't really all that good. It's actually pretty bad sometimes."

"Well, this is good," she says with her mouth full as we enter my room. Mickey's there, sitting on the floor by my bed.

Lacey stops chewing. "What are you guys doing?"

"We're drawing in my colouring books. I brought different kinds for you and Red, like this one here." Mickey opens a colouring book with stickers in it and portraits of Minnie Mouse and Donald Duck. "Disney," he tells her, and flips a few pages for her to see.

"I want that one! I want it, Mickey."

"I knew she'd like it," he says, arranging his glasses. "I knew it, Red. I told you so."

"You did, Mickey."

I give him his plate of lemon pie. Lacey's already on the floor, lying on her tummy with her hand in the pencil kit. She takes out a green crayon and starts colouring Minnie's bow.

"I'm doing what she's doing," Mickey says, and lies on the floor like Lacey.

Since he's copying Lacey, I have to do the same, and now we're all lying down together. I'm closer to the pillow, Mickey's closer to the foot of the bed, and Lacey's between us. After a minute or so, she says, "Yours is real nice, Mickey. I like the yellow and red on your dragon."

She turns to my drawing. "That's very green."

"It's a green rabbit," I tell her.

"Yeah."

She picks up a red crayon and goes back to her Minnie. I don't see what's wrong with my colour choice. She didn't say anything bad, but I know she doesn't like it. I thought she'd say, *It's nice*, or, *That's so cool*, or something like that 'cause my rabbit is green, her favourite colour. I think it's cool. Maybe I should give it violet eyes and blue feet. Blue ears.

For a while all we do is colour and eat in silence, checking each other's work from time to time like I usually do when I'm at school, in art class. And then all of a sudden Lacey says, "Cara wanted to come."

"What did you say to her?" I ask.

"I said you didn't invite her. She looked a little sad. I wanted to bring her along, but I didn't. I feel bad about leaving her."

"Only us three."

"Why not her?"

"'Cause." I raise the blue crayon from the page. "'Cause I only invited you and Mickey."

"Can she come next time?"

"I guess. If you want her to. But, you know, she never invited me to her place."

"Me neither," Mickey says. "She only invites you."

"That's true," she says, reaching for the black crayon. "Sometimes she can be a bit bossy."

"Can I have some more lemon pie?" Mickey asks me.

"Yeah."

"And some milk?"

"Yeah. You know where the glasses are?"

"I think so."

"Can I have some milk, too?" Lacey asks.

"Can you get some for her, too, Mickey?"

"Okay."

Mickey gets up and leaves the room, taking his plate with him. So far Lacey's taken only two bites of her lemon pie. Maybe she's too busy drawing to know it's still there. Her Minnie looks girly and pretty just like her. She's colouring each body part slowly, controlling the crayon to keep it from going over the black curvy lines. I'm not as careful as she is. My rabbit has green above its face and blue above its ears.

"Yours is real good," I tell her. "Much better than mine. You should give her brown eyes."

"Why's that?"

"So she can have a part of you."

She smiles at me and says, "Okay. I'll do that."

"Can I ask you something?"

"Yeah," she says, and goes back to her drawing.

"Do you and Cara talk a lot about us?"

"Us?"

"Like, everyone."

"Sometimes."

"Even me?"

She doesn't answer. I want to know the truth if it's a yes, but I also don't want to if it's a no or a yes. I think I'd rather know than not know, so I ask her again, even if Mickey's back in the room, listening.

"Even me?"

"Yeah," and then, "but Cara does most of the talking. She likes you, but you can't tell her that. She says you're nice and cute. But if I talk about you, she'll say bad things. It's like she doesn't want me to like you."

"What does she say?" I ask. "What does she say about me?"

"She says stuff like 'he's a troublemaker' or 'he doesn't like you that way' or 'he doesn't find you that pretty.' Stuff like that."

"I never said these things about you. They're just lies. Tell her, Mickey."

"He's right. Red would never say that. He thinks... It's true, what he says."

"I only have good things to say about you."

"I forgot the milk," Mickey says, and walks back out of the room.

"She's just jealous, Red."

"Still," I tell her, "it's not right."

"Maybe she doesn't mean what she says. Some people are like that."

"Some people, yeah. But Cara... She's hard to read."

I sign my name at the bottom of the page. With Cara's lies now in the air, I don't feel like colouring another animal. I feel like doing nothing, but I keep this to myself; otherwise I'll ruin their fun. Mickey comes back with the milk, and soon after that I hear the front door open then close. It's Ma. She's here. I get up and tell Lacey and Mickey to stay put.

"Redmond?" Ma shouts.

"Yeah! I'm coming."

I walk out of my room and see her in the living room, pouring herself a drink. She's sitting on the couch, looking exhausted and fed up as always. And now she brings her glass to her lips and tips her head back, emptying it in one quick gulp. Her hand reaches for the cigarette pack lying on the coffee table.

"Ma."

Without turning to face me she asks, "How was your day, honey?"

"Great, Ma. Lacey and Mickey are here."

"What?"

"They're here. I invited them over. They're in my room."

She lights a cigarette and takes a puff at it and pours herself another drink. I can't tell whether she wants to be alone or not. If we start making noise, she might snap at me or scare my friends away. She might do both, I think, so I don't take a chance.

"I'll tell them to go. I'll go, too, Ma."

She turns to me. I'm standing still, staring at her but not blinking. For a moment everything in the room is dead still— everything but the ribbon of smoke swirling up from her cigarette. Now her lips are curling a little on one side.

"Go," she says, almost whispering, and looks away. "Be back before six for supper, okay?"

"Okay."

I go back to my room and come back out with Lacey behind me and Mickey behind Lacey.

"Hi, Vicky," they both say.

"How are you guys doing?"

"Fine," Mickey says with a shy smile, swinging the grocery bag with all of his things in it.

"You look real pretty, Lacey," Ma says, smiling at her.

"Thanks, Vicky."

"Okay, we're going, Ma."

Lacey and Mickey walk to the front door. They'll go to the park without me. "I'll see you there," I tell them. As soon as they leave, I go to the living room and sit down next to Ma and hug her. She hugs me back.

"Go on," she says, rubbing my back, her head leaning against mine.

"I love you, Ma."

"I know, honey," she says, her voice soft like the wind. "I know."

35

I wake up from a deep sleep. The curtains are halfway open, but not much sunlight is coming in. Without leaving the bed, I stretch my legs and yawn. The alarm clock on my nightstand reads nine forty-seven. I hear a dog barking, distant voices shouting, but not Cara. She must be reading or writing in the living room. I pull the blanket over my head and yawn again, too tired and groggy to start the day. Lacey's leaving soon, in about an hour. Before we parted ways yesterday night she gave me her New York phone number. She still hasn't left, and I miss her already.

Half an hour later, I get up and walk out of the room. I stop just outside the doorway. Cara's sitting at the dining room table with a glass of orange juice in front of her, staring at something straight ahead, or at nothing at all.

"Morning," I say.

Rubbing my eyes, I enter the kitchen. Cara doesn't reply. I open the fridge and grab the pint of chocolate milk and pour myself a glass. (There's Lacey, a mental flash of her, as I set the pint on the counter.) I lift the glass to my mouth, feeling a cool, refreshing breeze seep in through the kitchen window, hearing the morning birds call to each other. I turn to Cara, smelling danger.

"What?" I ask softly. "What is it?"

Seconds pass. Neither of us speaks. I know what she's thinking, and I have a feeling she wants me to spit it out. She looks so serious with her arms crossed like a judge. Soon her eyes change expression, and all I see on her face is a picture of sadness.

"Cara."

She lowers her head. Tears are gathering in her eyes. I'm unsure at this point whether I should apologize now or later, whether I should say anything at all or wait for her to speak her mind.

"I'm sorry."

"Are you really?" She shakes her head and says, "I don't think so."

"I never wanted to hurt—"

"Oh, but you did. You certainly did."

My hand is shaking, so I put the glass on the counter. Silence intervenes again but not for long.

"This moment—*this*, you and me—I've played it out countless times in my head," she says, smiling for a second, "thinking about what to say to you, what you'd say to me, how we'd react. I thought I'd lash out at you. I thought I'd make you feel miserable, make you regret it all, all of it. I thought I would, Red, but I don't have the strength. I'm so tired." She stops and cries. "I'm tired of everything, of *you*... As you know from my diaries—'cause you *did* read them without my consent—I always wanted you to be mine. But you never really were, after all. You never were."

My mouth opens, but the words I want to say won't come out. The knot in my throat keeps thickening. The words won't come out.

"I loved you, Red. Despite everything, I loved you, with all of me."

Cara gets up and walks toward me until we're facing each other in the kitchen, in the morning light. Then something unexpected happens: She steps forward, opens her arms, and hugs me. She hugs me. I wrap my arms around her, and for a short while we remain that way—in that shocking, gentle embrace, our saddest one, the very last one. When we finally let go of each other, she heads over to the kitchen sink and looks out the window. Wiping away the tears, she says, "I don't want you here right now. I want you to leave."

"Cara."

"Just go."

"I'm sorry. I—"

"Don't talk to me. Just go! Get out!"

I go back to my room and put on my pants, my shirt, my shoes, trying my best not to break down. When I leave the room Cara's nowhere in sight, but the bathroom door is shut. I step out of the apartment, out of the building, and into the open air.

The morning birds are still here, idling on roofs and branches, taking flight. I keep walking, wanting nothing more than to go away like the birds, far away from this storm of negative energy. To avoid thinking about Cara, about us back at the apartment. And to be alone.

When I reach the local post office I decide, on impulse, to go downtown. I'm taking my time, passing a block of old apartment buildings facing a children's park, passing a group of kids, an elderly couple, a black cat. Later, while crossing a main street, I spot my school's principal stepping out of a grocery store with a plastic bag in each hand, walking away from me. The fact that he doesn't know I'm here brings me much relief. I keep walking until I reach a small café I've always wanted to try.

A WOMAN IN A BLACK APRON stands behind the counter, putting pastries on a display shelf. I count a dozen wooden tables, all round, including two by the window. I order a coffee and chocolate croissant and head to one of the tables by the window—the farthest one from all the seated customers.

I let my gaze wander from the coffee cup to the people walking past me beyond the window glass. All my life I've never thought much about strangers. To me they've always been part of a background, kind of like buildings and lampposts—things you know are there but forget the moment you pass them. But now, sitting here alone, I wonder if that woman over there, in a bookshop across the street—I wonder if her life is just as twisted as my own or if it's worse. Maybe it's better, but is it always rosy? Without troubles? Without worry? Aren't we bound to have bad times every now and then? Isn't that what *normal* is? Is my life normal, then?

I spend so much time analyzing random strangers that I forget the coffee I've barely touched. When noon arrives, the café is almost packed. I don't leave, I don't want to leave, so

I order some lunch, another coffee, and a slice of lemon pie. Lunch hour turns into early afternoon then midafternoon. With heavy eyelids, I pillow my head on my arms and drift off to sleep.

"**Hello, sir. Sir?**"

I open my eyes and look up at the employee standing beside me. I unfold my arms from the table and straighten myself. "Sorry. I dozed off. What time is it?"

She checks her watch and says, "It's four fifteen. Would you like anything else?"

Already four fifteen. I ask for the bill, and within five minutes I'm back outside. Instead of going downtown as planned, I walk back home, thinking about what to say, what to do next.

When I reach the apartment building, I don't see Cara's car. I go in and take the stairs. To my surprise the apartment door is open. "Cara?" I say, closing the door behind me. "Cara?" She's not here. Neither are any of her books and papers. I walk into our bedroom. Drawers are open, a pillow is missing, and Cara's stuff—her clothes, her jewelry, her makeup—all of it's gone. Before leaving the room, I head over to the open closet, expecting to find nothing but bare hangers.

Lying about on the floor where her boxes once were are little pink socks and white toddler shoes, a pacifier, a colourful bib—baby items for the child we never had.

36

s he makes his way around a block he remembers vividly, the beggar finds a spot to urinate. It's up ahead, no more than a twenty-second walk. But I'm in no hurry to get there, he tells himself. So he eases his cart near a squirrel moving under the sidewalk's metal rail and reaches into his cart for bread. Taking out a slice, he begins to hear footsteps somewhere behind him. He breaks the slice into fragments, tosses a few of them onto the grass, and waits for the squirrel to snatch the closest piece. Though his eyes are locked on the rodent, he can't stop thinking about those heavy, unsettling footsteps fast approaching.

The beggar turns around seconds before the stranger catches up to him—a college student no doubt, minding his own business—and by chance notices one of his flip-flops (the one with the broken strap) lying a short distance away on the sidewalk.

The stranger ignores him, walks past him, and now the beggar reaches down for the matching flip-flop dangling from the cart by a knotted shoelace. Yes, he thinks, grabbing it for a moment. Yes, it would've been nice to go there; it would've been the perfect time, today, right now, it would've been perfect. He unties the knot and, after straightening himself, hurls the flip-flop toward its fallen counterpart. With the remaining bread stuffed into his mouth, the picture in his mind (of sand and water, a forest, a sunny sky) dissolving into nothing, he sets his cart back in motion.

When he arrives at his destination seconds later, he stations his cart along the sidewalk's metal rail and glances around him. No one's coming his way. No one's watching him from a window or a balcony. Two big pine trees stand between the metal rail and the wall of a low-roofed apartment building. So close are the trees to one another that their branches overlap.

Without further delay, he climbs over the metal rail and hides himself behind the trees, his back facing the brick wall. He unzips his pants, lowers the front of his underwear a little, and takes his cock out. His gaze shifts from the cluster of pine needles before him to his cock, which he's wiggling. If he keeps wiggling it, the urine will come out sooner, but if he hears the slightest human sound, nothing will happen. In a washroom stall he almost never waits. Out here, though, out in the open where nothing is private, he has to be patient. So the beggar waits a little longer, hearing only city noise and his own voice whispering, "Come on," over and over.

Then he feels it. He breathes a sigh of relief when he sees it, a jet of clear yellow crashing into the pine needles. He realizes, while urinating, that he's not alone. In a hurry he shakes off the remaining droplets and tucks his cock back into his underwear. Through the pine needle spaces, he can tell that the figure nearing his cart is a woman, and he's quite certain she won't take any of his things. Of course, why would she? he asks himself. Though he wants to get back to his cart, he's worried that if he does he might startle or frighten her. So he waits, hoping she doesn't slow down. She doesn't.

The beggar gets out of hiding. His bladder now relieved, he can focus his time and attention on where to go from here. First things first: In order to reach his final destination, he needs to be on the opposite side of the block. The beggar turns his cart around. As he retraces his steps, he can't help but think about Joey and the old lady, other people he's met on today's journey, and all of that food stored in his cart. Should he eat Lipton soup and bread for supper and a tangerine for dessert? Or maybe the tangerine tomorrow morning and some apple sauce later today? Before he can decide, his mind gets distracted by someone up ahead, approaching. Someone of no more than seven or eight years of age, with hair the colour of sand and eyes as green as olives. He comes to a standstill when the beggar passes him, then turns around and begins walking alongside the cart, riveted as he is by the heap of junk overloading the wire basket. Assuming the boy will lose interest at any moment and walk the other way, the beggar keeps going, pretending he doesn't notice him. But as soon as the boy puts his hand on the cart, the beggar comes to a halt. He looks down at those eyes so alive with wonder, so innocent and pure like his once were, and breaks the silence between them.

"Go on. Go play with your friends."

The beggar's about to push his cart when the boy asks, "What's in there?"

"Nothing that concerns you. Now go on, boy."

"Can I see?" he asks. "I want to see."

"There's nothing to see. It's just clutter."

"What about that?" The boy points at something on the side of the cart.

Convinced that the boy won't leave until he's satisfied, the beggar gives in with a heavy sigh and a headshake. He stations his cart along the sidewalk's metal rail and rummages through his junk for an item or two worth showcasing. He pulls out an instrument and a deck of cards. Once they're both seated on the rail, the beggar offers him the deck of cards and says, "If you want it, you can keep it."

"Okay."

"It's brand new. Never opened it."

The boy opens the box and takes out the cards. He starts flipping through them casually, then quickly, but slows down when he gets to the jacks and the queens, the kings and the jokers.

"I'm guessing you've never played a game."

The boy shakes his head.

"You know what this is?" the beggar asks, opening his hand to reveal the instrument.

"No."

"A harmonica. I haven't played anything in the longest time. Don't know if I still can."

He brings the harmonica to his lips, cupping it with his hands, and blows into the mouthpiece. The resulting sound leaves the boy spellbound. He blows into it again, only this time he opens his hands slowly, altering the sound.

"I want to try!" the boy says enthusiastically, but the beggar refuses.

"It's not clean, son. Have your parents buy you one for Christmas. Now let's see…" the beggar says, thinking of a simple tune the boy might like.

He presses the mouthpiece to his lips. Despite the blunders made here and there, he doesn't stop until he finishes the whole song. The boy doesn't clap.

"That's a strange song."

"Glad you liked it."

"Not really," the boy says, staring at the cart. "You have a lot of stuff."

"I guess so."

"What's that smell?"

The beggar laughs. "Old wrecks smell bad. What can I say?"

The beggar spots a few passersby across the street, but they pay him no mind.

"Where are your parents? Aren't they worried about where you are?"

"My parents let me go wherever I want. I'm not a baby anymore. And I live only a block away. That's not far."

"Kids these days," the beggar says under his breath. "Where were you going?"

"Nowhere." The boy switches his gaze from the beggar's eyes to the king of spades, from the king of spades to the beggar's cart. "What else do you have in there?"

"Nothing important."

"I don't believe you. There's a rabbit."

"A rabbit?"

The boy points at the stuffed animal in the cart. The beggar gets up, puffing from the effort, and plunges his hands into his things.

"This you mean," he says, holding the rabbit-dog by the neck as he walks back to the rail. "My mother gave him to me."

"What's it called?"

"Max. His name's Max." He looks down at it and strokes its head. "He's been my travelling companion ever since I… But yeah, he's very precious to me. I don't plan on ever parting with him. I'm sure you have things you want to keep."

"All of my toys."

"You can hold Max if you like."

The boy takes it and puts it on his lap. "I used to have a rabbit. Not a real one. It was blue."

"What happened to it?"

"I don't know. It just disappeared."

"That's too bad." The beggar rises to his feet. "I'd better get going. It's getting late."

The boy, still seated, gives him back the rabbit-dog and says, "But it's not even dark yet."

The beggar smiles. "It was nice chatting with you," he says, grasping the cart handle. "Just promise me one thing."

"Okay."

"Be nice to your parents. And take good care of them. Can you do that?"

"Yeah, I can do that. My name's Richy by the way. What's your name?"

"Enjoy the cards," the beggar says, and walks on.

The boy watches him recede and turn at the corner. This time, he doesn't go after him.

37

I'm sitting on the living room couch, waiting impatiently on the line. Since yesterday evening my mind has been all over the place. I can't stop thinking about Cara, about everything she said to me before she left; I can't stop no matter how hard I try to block her out. What I need is a dose of Lacey—*my* dose of happiness. I called her this morning, eager to hear her voice, but she didn't pick up. I hope nothing bad happened. I don't know what I'd do if—

Lacey: Hello?
Me: Lacey?
Lacey: Red! I'm so glad to hear your voice!
Me: How was the flight?
Lacey: It was good. All was good.
Me: I didn't call you yesterday evening. I figured you wanted a day to get back into things, but I was worried.
Lacey: About the flight?

Me: Yeah.

Lacey: Everything went well. Even the airplane food wasn't bad. It's great to be back in New York, though. To see all my stuff, especially my bed.

Me: Just bring it with you on the airplane and I'll get rid of mine. How does that sound?
          (And now we're both laughing.)

Me: Lacey, I… It's over with Cara. Since yesterday morning.
          (Lacey's silent.)

Me: She said what she wanted to say.

Lacey: How are you feeling? Are you okay?
          (There's Cara's face, her tears, our last embrace flashing before my eyes.)

Lacey: Red? Are you okay?

Me: Yeah.

Lacey: It's my fault.

Me: No, don't say that. She's gone now, for good. And she left me the apartment. We can keep it if you want, or we can move out. It's up to you.

Lacey: We'll see.

Me: You'll let me know when you'll be back?

Lacey: Yeah. It'll take some time, though. You'll have to wait a bit.

Me: I understand. I'll wait for you.

Lacey: If only you were with me in New York. You would so love it here, seriously. You wouldn't want to leave.

Me: I believe you.

Lacey: I'm starting tomorrow.

Me: Oh, your job. Yes. It'll be fine, Lacey. I'm not worried at all.

Lacey: I'm actually excited about it, even if it won't last.

Me: Lacey?

Lacey: Yeah?

Me: I thought about our next date.

Lacey: Already? Don't you think it's a little early?

Me: Of course not. We should go to the park—Emerald Park. We haven't been there in ages. We can have a picnic on the main mound.

Lacey: The main mound. Gosh, I have so many memories of that place.

Me: Do you remember that last day? The day you left?

Lacey: Yeah. It was sad, wasn't it?

Me: I took it real hard. I even cried about the whole thing.

Lacey: You did? I did, too.

Me: I cried for days. I didn't want Ma to see me, but she caught me crying in the living room. I remember feeling embarrassed in front of her. And you know what she said? She said she always knew I liked you.

Lacey: How?

Me: She said I'd call for you in my sleep, that's how. After you left, I went back to the kissing tree a few times, when no one was watching.

Lacey: The kissing tree! That tree!

Me: The bridge. Kick-the-can. The flat-stone mound. We have to go back there, Lacey. We have to.

Lacey: We should.

(She's not alone: There's another voice on her end.)

Lacey: Wait a sec… Red? I have to go.

Me: Okay.

Lacey: But I'll talk to you soon.

Me: Lacey. Lacey, please say you're coming back.

Lacey: I am. I promise.

Me: I miss you.

Lacey: I miss you, too, Red. I'll talk to you soon.

38

The wind is blowing through my hair, drying the sweat on my skin. I feel like I'm driving on the highway, shooting past everyone and everything, moving so fast no one can catch me, not even Finn, who's running after a Frisbee. Many of us are in the park, scattered a bit everywhere. I'm the only one biking. I'm riding on the path leading up to the bridge, where Aaron is playing with his action figurines, and since I'm not in the mood for that kind of playing I pass him without stopping. I keep going straight and check on Lacey's progress. She's squatting at the base of the main mound, plucking a dandelion from the grass and adding it to the bouquet she's holding with her other hand. She told me earlier that she wants to give her mother something nice for her birthday. I think it's nice. The Frisbee is in the air again, flying past her, and there's Rex running after it, running fast but not fast enough. It lands on the grass before he can grab it.

"You wanna play, Red?" he asks me. "You want to or not? You, me, and Finn."

I tell him, "Not right now," and pedal on, against the wind.

Soon I'm out of the park, biking around the block among houses and big bushes, skinny trees all yellow-green, and then in no time at all I'm back with them, I see them: Alf coughing near the bridge, Aaron laughing, Rex crying out, "Get it! Get it!" and Finn shouting after catching it between his legs. I look straight ahead. My feet stop pedalling, my butt gets off the seat, and now I'm standing forward, turning the handlebars a little to the left, a little to the right, to the left again as I approach the next corner. After making two trips around the park, I see Cara opening her backyard door. Instead of biking toward her, I cut through the park and bike toward Mickey, who's checking his Marvel card collection by his backyard door.

If Cara thinks I'm going to say hi to her, she's wrong. And I won't apologize, either. She stole all the fun I had when Lacey and Mickey were drawing with me in my room. Everything was going well until Cara's lies leaked into my ears and got me angry. Lacey told me not to say anything, but when we were all in the park later that afternoon, I couldn't keep my mouth shut.

Cara came out a few minutes after we arrived, and when she joined us on the bridge, I called her a liar to her face. At first she pretended not to know what I was talking about, but then Mickey said Lacey had told us everything earlier that after-noon. Cara got angry at Lacey for sharing their secrets with us and said I was a bad influence on her and a loser. "No one likes you!" she said. I knew she was lying 'cause Mickey and Lacey like me and she does, too; she just doesn't want to admit it. So I called her a liar again and said, "You don't deserve Lacey as a friend. You think you're better than everyone, but you're not. No one cares about you, so go home."

She turned around and ran home. I'm not sure if she cried, though, and we've been avoiding each other ever since. She's with Lacey at the moment, helping her pick dandelions, talking to her about something. What if she turns Lacey against me? What if she tells her new lies about me? If I could keep Lacey away from Cara all day long, I would. More than anything, I wish they were no longer friends. I get off my bike and leave it on the grass.

"I got new cards," Mickey says as I take a seat next to him.

There's Alf coming toward us with a box between his hands. I look down at Mickey's cards. The drawings are real cool, all different from each other. Mickey says he needs a few more cards to complete his collection. He used to buy a pack every week with his father's change. Now he just wants to trade some of his doubles and triples for the cards he still doesn't have. Ma says they're nothing more than a piece of cardboard. Maybe she's right, or maybe she's lying to avoid paying for something she can't really afford. There's only one card I have. One of Mickey's doubles. A while back Mickey wanted me to take all of his doubles, but I told him I only wanted the Sub-Mariner 'cause he can live underwater and fly. Alf sits down beside him and opens his box.

"I got some new ones," Alf says. "Wanna trade?"

"Depends," Mickey says. "I want to see."

They swap their pack of doubles and flip through them quickly while my eyes move back and forth from one pack to the other, from Thor and his hammer to Wolverine and his claws to Captain America and his big bullseye shield and so on.

After a while I get bored and hop back on my bike. Hank's on his balcony, calling for Finn to come over. Finn tosses the Frisbee at Rex and disappears behind Hank's backyard door, leaving Rex all by himself. Soon everyone will go home to eat, and when they'll come back out, they'll want to play kick-the-can. Chances are I'll be the seeker. But today I don't feel like playing games. What I really want is to ride around the neighbourhood with my friends, if they're willing.

I have some change tucked in my pocket. Ma gave it to me this morning. Said I earned every coin for doing my chores and helping her out, like when I wash the dishes and sweep the floor. If I want I can put the money into my piggy bank, but I'd rather spend it on candy today.

Lacey's not outside. She must've gone back home with her dandelions. I follow the path toward the bridge, and when I stop by Lacey's backyard I see her family there, through the gaps between the fence boards. Her mother's speaking. Forks and knives are hitting plates. I step on my pedal and give myself a push, but a voice stops me.

"Red," Lacey says, looking at me with one eye between two fence boards. "Red."

I get off my bike and walk up to her.

"What's going on?" she says while chewing.

"Nothing."

"I'm eating by the way."

"Yeah, I know. Are you coming back out?"

"I think so. Probably."

"You want to bike after?" I hear a hand banging on Lacey's backyard table and some grown-up laughter.

"I don't know," she says, her eye disappearing then reappearing. "I might have to stay here a while 'cause it's my mom's birthday."

"Yeah, okay. I'll ask Mickey and we'll ring at your door. If your mother answers, I'll ask her."

"If you want."

"She'll say yes, I'm sure."

"Okay, go eat," she says. "I'll wait."

So I go back home as fast as I can. I catch Ma in her room, folding clothes. I tell her I want to eat early, I want to eat right away, and she says, "Okay. There's some leftover stew in the fridge." Usually a meal takes me only about fifteen minutes to finish, so I don't rush, I try not to. I hope Lacey's still in her backyard or waiting for me in her house. If she's out in the park, she'll stick with Cara, and I don't want Cara to bike with the three of us. Why should she be with us anyway? She's not a nice person.

I leave my empty plate in the sink and go back outside with my bike. I'm not pedalling fast 'cause my tummy is full, and Ma says we should never move around too much after a meal; otherwise we might feel sick afterward or even throw up.

When I get to the park, Mickey's not there. Lacey isn't, either. Alf, Rex, and Cara are playing Frisbee while Aaron's sitting in front of Mickey's backyard, checking out Alf's Marvel cards. I pass through an alleyway and go straight to Mickey's. I leave my bike on the ground and walk up the front steps. His father answers the door.

"Red!" he says, almost shouting. "Mickey's eating."

Where did all of his hair go? He used to have some on his head.

"Okay, sir. I...I was wondering if he can come back out after he's done eating."

"Red?" Mickey shouts from somewhere behind his father. "Red!"

Mickey appears beside his father in the doorway. "Yeah, Red, I'm coming out. I'm almost done."

His father leaves, and then I say, "Can you take your bike out when you're ready?"

"My bike? Finn said we'd play kick-the-can."

"Forget him, Mickey. Forget all of them."

"Finn wants you to be it. What a jerk, eh?"

"Let's just go. With Lacey."

"Oh, yeah?"

"We'll be three."

"Fine. I'll be out in a sec, okay?"

"Okay."

I wait for him down below, next to his parents' car. A few minutes pass, and then his garage door opens. Mickey comes out with his bike, and off we go to Lacey's.

"Where do you want to go after we pick up Lacey?" he asks, in back of me.

"You'll see."

"Have I been there before?"

"Yeah. You've been everywhere I've been, Mickey. But you'll like it."

We don't ring at Lacey's door. She's already outside with her bike parked by her side, and she's wrapping a colourful bracelet around her ankle.

"Lacey!" I shout.

"I'm ready," she says. "Took you guys a while."

"Yeah, sorry." I slow down, but I don't stop. "Stay behind Mickey."

"Where are we going?"

"He won't tell us," Mickey says. "Where do you think he'll take us?"

"Don't know. That's why I'm asking."

"We'll be there soon," I tell them.

Mickey figures it out 'cause he says, "The dépanneur. He's bringing us to the dépanneur, I know it. I just know it," and in less than a minute we're already there.

We lean our bikes against the glass of the store, and Mickey pushes the door open. Tony's behind the counter with a newspaper between his hands. He doesn't know Mickey and Lacey very well, so he only says hi to me.

"I don't have money, Red," Mickey says behind my ear.

"Me, neither," Lacey whispers beside me.

"I know. That's why I brought money." I pull out my change.

Tony looks down at the coins I put on the counter. "With that amount," he says, "you can get yourself two dozen candy."

Does he mean two plus twelve or two times twelve? He's not very clear.

"How much is that?" I ask.

"Twenty-four. That's eight for each of you," he says, his eyes peeking over his glasses. "Tell you what, take ten each. How does that sound?"

"That sounds good."

We're all excited now. I only want toffee, so I take ten toffee race cars. Like Mickey, Lacey takes all kinds of candy. Tony puts them into three paper bags for us. When I give him the money, he says, "Say hi to your mother for me, okay?"

"Okay. Thanks, Tony."

Mickey and Lacey thank him, too, and we leave the dépanneur with our paper bags in our pockets. Once we're back on our bikes, Mickey asks me where I want to go next. Not the park, I tell him.

"Let's go to the front of your house."

"If you say so," he says, and takes the lead.

Like Marvel's Quicksilver, we get there in a flash. We take a seat on the stairs leading up to Mickey's front door. Mickey sits on the third step while Lacey and me sit on the first. We start eating our candy, not saying a word, just eating and looking around. The sun's making the sky orangey, and across the street the tree leaves are singing, stirring a little.

"Thanks for the candy," Mickey says.

"It's fine, Mickey."

"Can I have a race car?"

"You didn't get any?"

"I thought I did. But no."

I turn around and let him take a race car. I figure Lacey may want one, too.

"Do you want one, Lacey?"

"No," she says, chewing a strawberry-shaped jujube. "I have one already."

"Can we stay here a while?" I ask them.

"Yeah," Mickey says. "We can do that."

"Mmm…" Lacey turns to me, still chewing. "This is a real good jujube! Thanks, Red," she says, and puts her hand on my hand.

39

It's not easy living alone. Apart from eating and watching TV, I don't do much of anything, really. I don't like to read or draw, so my hobbies at home are pretty limited. If there's one aspect I like about solitude, it's the silence that welcomes me after a full day's work. No whys or you-shoulds or when-will-yous. Just peace and quiet.

Nine months. That's how long it's been now since Cara left. For a while I thought she'd come back and try to make amends, but she hasn't come back, not once. Part of me was hoping she would so I could see her again, hoping because maybe I—I guess I miss her in a way, despite everything.

In the days following the breakup, I pretended Cara was still with me in the apartment. I thought about all the things I would've liked to say to her. Things that would've hurt her, angered her—my own truths. Sometimes I wonder (even now, after all this time) whether or not she's dating. I also wonder what my life would've been like had I not met Lacey at the bar.

It's midday. Yesterday's storm clouds are still drifting across the sky. The light is pale. A sickly white filtering through the curtains, striking the living room floor in long, slanted beams. Instead of watching the news I'm listening to the rain while eating broccoli and some leftover macaroni and cheese. So far this week I've done nothing eventful with my vacation time. Cara always wanted to do something big, like visit a neighbouring city for two or three days. She'd try to match her vacation weeks with mine, but this time everything is different: I can wake up when I want, go where I want, do nothing if I want. *Real* vacation. Lately I've been working longer hours to make ends meet. I'm already behind on the rent, and I have to cut certain grocery expenses like fast food and chocolate. I could always find a roommate if things go downhill, but I'd rather live with the person I love, and something tells me I'll never see her again. My Lacey.

Weren't we happy together? I was. I believed in us. I was so certain that everything would turn out as planned, but the opposite happened. Our phone conversations, which were frequent in the days following her departure last September, grew infrequent after the first month, then stopped completely by February. They stopped because she was no longer answering my calls.

Did I hurt her in some way? But how? I was forgiving. I was nice to her, committed to her. Did she really love me? If only I had answers. If I did, I wouldn't be sitting here making up so many scenarios in my head. At first I was angry at her, then depressed, and now I'm sure I did something wrong. She's still very much alive in my mind, but for how long I can't say.

Putting my plate into the sink, I find myself thinking about a talk I had with a gym teacher at the school the other day.

He told me writing helps to relieve stress and anxiety. I'm not so sure if that's true (nor am I keen on anything that involves writing), but I certainly have nothing to lose by testing it out.

I set a glass of grape juice on the dining room table and search for a notepad and a pencil. I find a pen and some loose-leaf paper in my drawer and take a seat at the table. The teacher suggested I write what I'm feeling and thinking in the present. I start off with *June 27th 1994* on the first line and *The day is rainy and gloomy* on the second, followed by:

> *Bad weather keeps my spirit's down. Cara likes rain. She once said it would calm her and was refreshing to her. She hurt me bad but I hurt her to, and now we are hurting. I always loved Lacey. I know that for sure. Back when we were just kids, Cara would act all know it all, like she was better than all of us. I hated that about her, at the time I hated it. No. It is not true. I hated seeing her and Lacey together. But looking back I understand why, I think. If a boy was in love with Lacey I would try to keep them apart. I guess I'm no different than Cara. Some times I wish I never met Lacey. Not knowing her means no agonie, no sadness and no hurting either, not all this waiting around. Most times I'm glad I met her. She is part of me. And if she comes back we'll start over. I'll let her live with me if she wants to, and we'll start over without having to cover any tracks. The whole time I was with her I was happy. I felt alive. I*

hope she was alive like me. I wonder what she is doing. Maybe it is raining over in New York also. She once said to me she likes going out on rainy day. She said long ago when she was just a kid she'd go on her balcony and let the rain fall on her and soke her to her toes. The first time I saw Lacey was in the park. Ma and me were new to the neighbourhood, and one day I was walking around with Ma, and we were exploring the neighbourhood. And just like that she was there playing with a doll all alone on the grass looking pretty. I was very young, but even at that age she took my breath away. I love you

I put the pen down. Writing the first sentences was tough, but then all of these ideas came rushing out of my head like a waterfall, and all I wanted to do was write the next sentence, then the next, and so on. I feel a bit better now, more calm in the heart, less worried in the mind. I get up from the chair and go to the closest window. The rain is beating down the street like thousands of glass beads. Lacey would've gone out without hesitating, I'm sure of it. I go straight to my room, strip off my clothes, and put on a pair of shorts and a white undershirt. I take my keys with me and open the door. As soon as I step outside the apartment building barefoot, I feel them—so many drops on my face and shoulders, wetting my undershirt, sliding down my skin like streams on a slope. I get to the sidewalk but see no one in either direction, no cars in motion. Suddenly a lightning bolt rips open the sky. I can feel my heart racing and I'm afraid, I'm afraid but too thrilled to go back inside and hide, so I start running.

By the time I reach the next block my clothes are soaking wet and sticking to my skin. I keep going. Soon I pass three men leaving the dépanneur in a hurry, each one with a case of beer cans under one arm. Two or three streets later, I come across a couple in yellow raincoats jogging, a woman with grocery bags running from her driveway up to her porch, a dog spying on me from a window. The wind is getting stronger, the trees more restless. Before long I stop at a four-way intersection. There's a short queue of people waiting at a bus stop across the street, all of them watching me under their umbrellas. So many cars are zooming past us from both sides, making swishing sounds with all of that rain building up on the ground, and now they're slowing down, slowing until only their wipers are moving. I wipe the rain from my eyes and run straight ahead toward the traffic light and the umbrella people, not looking back, not knowing where I want to go, but feeling free.

After a minute or two the rain and the wind die down and I make for a small underpass. A dark blue car drives past me, then slows down and stops within seconds. I'm about to pass the car when someone shouts my name.

I stop near the open window and lower my head and look in. Red hair. Brown eyes. Freckles. I recognize her right away. She works in the school cafeteria.

"Oh, Frances. How's it going?"

"Good!" she says, from the other side of the car. "Do you need a ride?"

"No, I'm okay. But thanks."

"You sure?" She glances at her rear-view mirror. "And where are your shoes?"

If only I'd seen her coming I would've chosen another route. To avoid an explanation I answer, "I'll see you at school. Thanks again."

"See you at school, then," she says, and rolls the window back up.

Off she goes, to the other side of the underpass. Instead of following her I make a right before the underpass, then head for Marigold Park a few streets away. When I get there, I take the path that cuts diagonally through the block. The trees here are taller than three-storey houses; some are so close to the path they act as oversized umbrellas, a shield of dark greens. As I make my way to the other end, images of the past, of my own childhood, suddenly flood my vision. Images of Lacey and me on the grass, watching the clouds float by, sitting face to face on the bridge, hiding in the bushes, just us. I can't go on, so I stop more than halfway across the block and let the tears go—tears of loss, tears of guilt, of sadness, hot tears. I step off the path and sit down under a tree with my back against the trunk and my knees drawn up. I look at the raindrops falling and disappearing on the path, on rooftops—just letting the tears go as I sit there, thinking about the people I love. The people I've lost.

40

Ma's on sick leave. She's been undergoing treatment for some time, trying not to give up, not to give in. I keep telling her to stay strong, but I don't think I'm all that convincing. At school I find it hard to concentrate. My teachers know about Ma's sickness, so they're real sympathetic, but I don't want their sympathy. I want Ma to be healthy. I want her to live longer than me.

For the last few weeks, Ma's been staying at the hospital. Her condition has gotten worse. Every day after school, I visit her at the hospital. Cara's been spending more time with me. She says I shouldn't be alone when bad things happen. Last Friday she came with me to the hospital, and the two of them chatted like they were great pals. Ma's known her for a long time, and she likes her very much. She thinks we make a cute couple, and I agree with her.

When Ma told me she was dying, I couldn't believe it. I *refused* to believe it. 'Cause all I ever had was Ma, and without Ma I'd be left with nothing. She kept on talking and talking, but my mind wasn't there anymore—*I* wasn't there anymore. All I could hear was her voice trembling, not her words. Later that day, while Ma was at work, I cried my heart out and thought about her suffering, not looking like herself, about never seeing her again. I'm scared. Every day now, I'm scared.

I'm at the hospital, taking the stairs. Ma's on the fifth floor, in a room she shares with another patient. There's always some action in the corridors, nurses and visitors coming and going, when I arrive and when I leave. I get to Ma's room and see her there, sleeping. The window is partly open, letting some of that springtime, summerlike hotness pass through. I put the flowers I bought for Ma into a pot on the windowsill and take a seat next to her. I try not to wake her as I unzip my school bag. She's not stirring. Her mouth is open, her breathing noiseless. She wakes up when I finish most of my math homework.

"Redmond," she whispers, looking at me like I'm a birthday present.

"How was your day, Ma?"

"It was fine."

"How do you feel?"

"I'm okay."

"Yeah?"

"Yeah. It's hot today. It's so hot."

"For sure. It's like summertime."

"What's that?" she asks, her eyes widening. "Is that for me?"

"Just for you."

"They're beautiful. You didn't have to."

"I can bring the flowers closer."

"No, leave them there. Give them some light. Have you been here a while?"

"Thirty minutes."

"Will you stay with me?" she asks. "Will you stay a bit longer?"

"Of course, Ma."

"Only if you can. If you have to go—"

"I'm not leaving, Ma. I'm staying if you want me to."

She looks relieved. "Did you eat yet?"

"No. I'll get something in the cafeteria. I can get you something."

"No, I'm fine. I'm just tired, that's all."

"Rest, Ma. I'll be right here."

"No, no, it's fine. I miss being with you, honey. I miss my bed. It's hard to sleep with all the noise in the corridor. And I feel weaker and weaker. I'm scared."

"I know, Ma. I'm scared, too."

"I never wanted this for you," she says, her eyes moist.

"Did you see the doctor? Did he come today?"

"Not yet. Redmond," she says, holding my hand. "Redmond, I want you to listen to me. You need to be strong."

"Ma."

"That's what I want. I don't want to go, but if that happens, you have to be strong."

"You're not leaving. You can't." My voice is breaking. "I won't allow it, Ma. You have to fight it."

"I know, honey."

"I don't think I can go on if... That's why you're gonna get through it."

"I'm doing the best I can."

"I know, Ma. I—"

"I'm trying, but I feel so weak. It's so hot today, don't you find? It's so hot."

"Do you want some water?"

She nods, so I take her cup of water and tilt it toward her open mouth, touching her forehead, her cheek.

"You're hot, Ma. I can put a wet cloth on your forehead."

"No, that's fine."

"You sure? It will only take a second."

"It's fine, honey, but thanks."

I sit on the bed next to her and hold her hand. "I was talking to one of my friends at school the other day. His mother—she's good friends with a vice-principal at an elementary school. Apparently he's looking to hire a janitor."

"Oh, yeah?"

"Yeah. I was thinking maybe I should apply for the job. Work in the summer maybe, if he'll have me."

"It must be a full-time position, not just a summer job."

"I guess so. It's something I wouldn't mind doing."

"Apply, then. You have nothing to lose."

"I'll apply, Ma."

"I'm so proud of you."

"Why?"

"Just am. I want you to know that. I've been thinking a lot about things I've done lately. There's not much to do here, not much I can do. Can you be honest with me?"

"Yeah."

"Was I ever good to you, honey? Was I?"

"Yes."

"You really mean that?"

I nod. I smile a little. "You didn't have it easy, Ma, but you did the best you could. I knew that, back then. I knew you did the best you could. You weren't always easy to be around, though."

"I know. I'm sorry. Do you forgive me?"

"There's no need, Ma. No parent is perfect—no parent. We all make mistakes. I'm glad I'm yours, Ma. I'm glad. You did the best you could. You did good." Sniffling, blinking quickly, I smile and say, "You should rest, Ma. I'll let you rest."

"Okay."

"I'll get something to drink. You want something?"

"No, I'm fine. Go ahead."

"I'll be right back. I'm not going anywhere."

"I know, honey. I know."

"Rest a bit, Ma."

"Okay."

I walk out of the room and make my way to the vending machine, unable to hide my sadness. I look around. There's no place to cry without being seen, so I walk back to Ma's room with a Sprite and sit down again. Ma's eyes are closed. She's breathing slowly. She's breathing. My emotions are getting the better of me, but I can't help it.

Leaving the Sprite can on the chair, I get up and go to the window. I put my hand over my eyes, trying not to make a sound.

"Red?"

Cara's in the room, walking toward me. She puts her school bag on the floor and hugs me. "Red, it's okay. I'm here," she says as I wrap my arms around her, my face buried in her shoulder. "I'm here."

If I could switch places with Ma, I'd do it, of course I would. It just breaks my heart to see her this way. I can't even do anything to help her, to make her sickness go away, *Don't go. Please don't go, Ma, Ma, I love you.*

FOR THE NEXT WEEK I laughed with Ma, cried with her, held her in my arms. And then it happened. My ma, Vicky, died on a Friday morning at eight twenty. I wasn't there to say goodbye, to be by her side in her final hours. It's been only two days since she passed away, and I miss her so much.

She was only forty-one.

41

Like anyone in love, I waited. Ma once said love is blind. At the time, I didn't quite understand the meaning of those words. I was too young, too naïve to understand. But now I do.

In the end Lacey didn't come back to me; she didn't keep her promise. Many people turn to their fridge or their bed when they're down or lonely. I turn to alcohol. The more I drank, the less I wanted to stop, and since I had no one to stop me I just kept on drinking. Several times a week I'd go to the bar, *that* bar, hoping to find her there. Like a fool, I waited.

Then one day someone at my school told the principal I "smelled heavily of alcohol." It wasn't like I was drunk or anything. I wasn't behaving weird, either, or hurting anybody. I told the principal I'd taken only a few sips of liquor, but he wasn't convinced. He gave me a warning, and I went home that day in shock. I opened the apartment door, went straight to the kitchen, and took out a beer from the fridge. Then I went back out to meet the sun, walked all the way to the canal, sat down on a bench along the bike path, and drank. I didn't know what else to do, so that's what I did. I thought of nothing; I felt nothing but calm. Maybe at that point I just didn't care anymore. Even now, lying sideways on the grass, smoking in the shade, I find myself not caring much about anything.

It's almost noon—almost lunchtime. For the past hour I've been doing nothing but yawning and daydreaming, watching people. As much as I'd enjoy taking a nap, the Chinatown noise from across the street won't let me, not to mention all the traffic at this hour. Here comes Cormer with his huge backpack, saluting me with a nod.

"Cormer."

"What's up?" he asks.

"Nothing much. Barely slept yesterday. Don't know why. You?"

"Nothing much, either."

He's lying next to me on the grass, with his head propped on his backpack, his arms crossed over his chest.

I pass him my cigarette. "How was last night?"

"Last night?" He pauses to puff a cloud of smoke. "Hung out with some guys I know. We had a shitload of booze, so I can't complain. It was awesome," he says, giving me back my cigarette.

Cormer's a great friend. We're almost the same age, and we always help each other out. Cormer had left his mother's home a week before I moved out of my apartment, the difference being that he'd wanted to, while I didn't. I got evicted because I couldn't pay the rent, and I couldn't pay the rent because I was unemployed and broke. Weeks before my eviction, I'd brought my foolishness to another level: I'd gotten drunk before going to work one morning, and this time several teachers noticed something strange in my behaviour and reported me. I was fired that day, fired after strike two, but what was I thinking? Why didn't I see this coming? I should've been more careful.

I left my apartment for good on a Friday. I took with me a backpack (which I stuffed with food, among other things), a rolled-up blanket, my wallet, my pocket money. Within days I started to beg, avoiding my former apartment building, my former workplace, afraid of being recognized by familiar faces. Eventually I found the homeless shelter where I met Cormer. I've been on the streets for about a year now. The past seems so distant whenever I think about it, like it was altogether a life different from my own, a life belonging to another person entirely. Sometimes I miss it, its flaws, the people who were part of it.

"Were you lucky today?" Cormer asks, borrowing my cigarette again.

"So-so."

I show him today's earnings. He reaches into his pocket and shows me up to twenty or thirty dollars in bills and change. Maybe it's the charm in his smile or his baby face or those dark green eyes of his that compel people to open their wallets, I don't know. He asks me if I've eaten and I say, "Only some crackers and the orange you gave me yesterday afternoon."

"I have a sandwich."

He turns over and kneels in front of his backpack. I watch him unzip the front pocket, and sure enough, there it is, half eaten.

"Here," he says, and without hesitating I take it. I thank him.

"Don't worry about it." He turns over and sits cross-legged with what remains of my cigarette. The wind is blowing gently through his long blond hair. He looks at me and says, "There's this guy I saw on Baker Street this morning. He wasn't using a cup or a baseball cap. He was holding up this fishing pole. Not a real one, though. He must've made it himself. A long wooden stick with a string attached to it, and a cup acting like bait, hanging from the string. I thought it was cool, man. For now I just have a cup. I can get a string at the dollar store, but the stick will be harder to get. I'm trying to find one, like a really long branch that won't easily crack."

"If I find one, I'll keep it for you."

"It's a good idea, eh?"

"For sure."

Once again Cormer lies flat on his back. He closes his eyes. Not knowing what else to say, I go on eating. The traffic light over there has turned green, and now half a dozen pedestrians are crossing with a bag of food in each hand, their arms hanging at their sides like taut ropes. I wouldn't be surprised if there's a takeout container of fried noodles in one of those bags, some shrimp dumplings, brown rice, oily vegetables—everything I like.

"What's on your mind?" I ask, having just swallowed the last mouthful of bread and ham.

His mouth opens but not his eyes. "The past."

I change position so that I'm lying on my back with the tree leaves above me dancing in the breeze.

"Sometimes I like listening to the wind blowing through the trees, making them whisper," he says. "It's that swishing sound. You hear it?"

"Yeah."

"That swish. Kinda reminds me of waves breaking on the shore. I used to hear that sound a lot. My parents—when they were still together, when Dad was still alive—they'd bring me to the beach on summer weekends. It's what they liked most, but not me. I'd tag along 'cause that's what kids do. It was way better than Sunday mass, but I kind of grew tired of it after a while. I just wanted to play with my friends or watch TV or sleep, you know? I don't think most kids realize how lucky they are. I certainly didn't."

Lifting my head a little, I notice his eyes are open, looking up.

"I'm picturing myself back there, in the water," he says, "floating with my face to the sky. It's nice. Feels nice. Now I'm swimming farther from the shore, letting the waves crash into my face. There's Mom with her black sunglasses, lying under a parasol, and Dad moving toward me in knee-deep water. When I want to break away from reality, I think about waves. They calm me, you know?"

All of this talk about the beach brings back old memories I'd rather keep hidden, even from myself. I get up and yawn.

"Leaving?" he asks.

"Maybe. Yeah."

"Where to?"

"I'm going for a walk. You can come if you like."

"Nah, I'll pass this time. I'll meet you at the shelter."

I sling my backpack over my shoulders and hit the road alone, trying to clear my thoughts. I come across a group of students sitting by the window of a café with their textbooks wide open. I'm about their age, but I'll never be what they'll be.

I'll never be a doctor, a teacher, a dentist, a businessman. Am I wasting my life? Is it too late for me to change?

"Wait up, Red!" says a voice from behind me. "Wait up!"

Turning around, I see Cormer catching up to me. "What are you doing?"

"Sorry, man. I got bored over there by myself. I figured you could use a bit of company."

Strange. While Cormer's talking about his plans for tomorrow, an image of Mickey—someone I haven't seen or spoken to in over a decade—crops up out of nowhere. I wonder how he's doing. If he even remembers me. Of all the kids I knew back then, he was one of the very few who never hurt me.

"You okay?" Cormer asks. "Something troubling you?"

"No…just thinking about someone I once knew from another life. We lost touch."

"I'm guessing that someone was your friend?"

"He was," I answer, feeling a small lump in my throat. "He was the best…my best friend."

42

Lacey told me the news last Monday, and since then I've been thinking about it every day. Even at the dinner table, or when I'm lying in bed waiting to fall asleep, I think about it. I don't like feeling sad, but I am. Just by looking at me, Mickey knew something was wrong. I spoke with him about it last Tuesday while we were walking to the dépanneur.

"She didn't tell me she was moving away," Mickey said, his eyes bigger than usual. "Otherwise I would've told you right away."

"I know, Mickey. I'm…I'm sad. It really sucks."

"Yeah."

"Why Lacey? Why not Hank or Finn? Or even Rex?"

"Don't know, Red. I guess things just happen."

"I hate that it's not one of them. I hate it."

"Do you know where she's going? Is it another city?"

"I didn't bother asking," and that's the truth. After she broke the news, the only question I wanted to ask was why she was leaving. So I asked her. She said her parents want to live in a "nicer" neighbourhood. I think that's a very stupid reason. Apart from the people I don't like, I see nothing wrong with our neighbourhood. Lacey was just as sad as I was about the news and just as shocked. But she's afraid. I told her it was normal to be afraid of going somewhere you've never been before and having to meet new people, but she still doesn't want to go, and I don't blame her. She also thinks we'll never see each other again. What if she's right? Ma says we make friends and lose them and make new ones over time. I'd rather keep my good friends than make new ones. I don't have many friends. Maybe that's why I feel so sad. If we were old enough to make our own decisions, Lacey and me would live at my place, with Ma. I'm sure Ma would be okay with the idea.

The other day I dreamed that it was my birthday. I was sitting at the dining room table, and Ma was standing close to me, singing. Even with Ma there, I kind of felt lonely without Lacey and Mickey singing along with her. Ma told me to make a wish, so I did. Taking a deep breath, I blew all the candles on my cake in one shot. That's when everything around me disappeared. Suddenly I was no longer at home; I was somewhere far away, sitting at the very top of a big hill. And there were other big hills, too, some looking more like round rectangles, others like round triangles. Lacey came up from behind me with a white birthday cake, followed by Mickey. Though their faces were blurry, I knew it was them. By their shape and voices, I just knew. It didn't matter that we were the only ones there eating the cake with our fingers, or that neither of them had presents for me. I didn't feel lonely or sad. I didn't want to leave. I thought everything was real, but when I woke up and realized it wasn't I tried to fall asleep again, to go back there, to go back to them. I wanted to, but I couldn't.

At school, boys never cry unless they're beaten up. I try not to cry 'cause that's what girls do, and I'm not a girl. Lying in bed, staring at the ceiling after the dream was over, I felt the tears coming. I felt them rolling across the side of my face, wetting my pillow. I never told anyone I cried that morning, not even Mickey.

Later during the day we were all in the park, and I was the seeker. Every time we play kick-the-can or any other game, part of me wants to win. But this time I didn't care. I wasn't alert; I wasn't trying, so one after the other, Hank, Finn, and Cara would run up to the soccer ball and kick it, and the game would start all over again. When we finally stopped playing, I found myself with Lacey, walking by her side on the grass.

"Do you know where you're moving to?" I asked her.

"Somewhere near my school," she said, twirling a flower between her fingers. "My dad said that you and Cara—everyone will leave this place eventually."

"I wasn't planning on leaving."

"He thinks you will."

"How does he know that?"

"I don't know," she said, moving her shoulders up and down. "But I think he's right."

"It's not gonna be the same, once you're gone."

"Do you really mean that?"

"Yeah. It's not gonna be the same. Last night I had a dream about us—you, me, and Mickey."

"Really?"

"We were on a hill, eating my birthday cake."

"You're also in my dreams."

"Oh, yeah?" I asked, surprised in a good way.

"Sometimes."

I expected her to go on about her dreams, but then her mother shouted, "Lacey! Supper's ready!" and so she left.

Two days have passed since then, and now it's Monday morning. Instead of waking up at ten or eleven, I woke up at seven. I had to. I tiptoed my way to the kitchen, where I made myself some breakfast—a bowl of cereal and a glass of milk—while Ma was still sound asleep. Lacey's leaving this morning. I promised I'd say goodbye to her in person, so I will. She said to come by no later than nine. The clock tells me it's eight forty-five. I guess I should be heading out soon, like in a minute or two. Ma will freak out if she doesn't know where I am, so I go back to my room for a sheet of loose-leaf paper and a pencil. Without sitting down at my desk, I grab the pencil and set the tip of it on the blank sheet, thinking about what to write, waiting, until finally the pencil begins to flow.

Hi Ma,

I am going out now. Dont worry I am ok. You can go to work. I love you Ma

Red

I take the note with me and leave it on the dining room table. To help out Ma, I clean the cereal bowl and the glass, wipe them dry, and put them back into their separate cupboards. Before I go, I pick something up from under my bed, something special to take with me, and in less than a minute I'm outside running under a bright sun.

All the way to the park I hear birds crying out, the wind blowing through the trees. When I arrive, I notice her backyard door is closed. I run up to the bridge, hoping she sees me there. Maybe she forgot about today. I could always ring her doorbell, but I'd rather wait a little. So I take a seat on the rail and wait. I start counting out loud, looking from time to time at her balcony door. The moment I reach fifty-eight, Lacey slides it open. She doesn't seem excited at all. She walks down the balcony steps and opens her backyard door. I wave at her as she walks up to me, her hair covered in sunshine, her lips almost smiling. Almost.

"Hey," I say as she sits down next to me on the rail.

She doesn't answer. Her eyes are looking down.

"You okay?"

"Not really. No."

"When are you leaving?"

"Very soon. The truck people are taking all the furniture out. There's not much left to do. I don't want to go, Red. I don't want to."

"I don't want you to go, either."

"Cara said she'll come visit me soon. You can come, too, if you want."

"Yeah, that would be cool."

"What's that?" she asks, her eyes pointing at the card between my hands.

"It's for you."

I made it myself using green construction paper, which I folded in half. Inside the card I drew a dog and a dolphin 'cause they're her favourite animals, and I also wrote her a message from the heart, in purple:

Lacey,

You are a great friend. I want you to know I
like you. Your very nice. And you smile. You look
like a princesse. I hope you will come back soon.
I want you to stay. You have to go and that is
no good. Your in my dreams and I'm in your
dreams to. We always have each other. I miss you

Red

Next to my name I drew a red heart with an arrow going through it. The letters I wrote were too big, so I had to write part of my message over and under my animal drawings and finish the rest on the back. I give her the card, unsure whether she'll like it or not. The front has blue and purple clouds on it with little houses below, and there's a big road curving like a rainbow, with me and Lacey walking on it, hand in hand.

"To Lacey," she says, reading the front page out loud.

She opens the card. She's reading it in her head now, so I wait, looking at her, wondering what she's thinking. After a while she puts the card down on her lap and smiles.

"Thanks, Red."

"I meant everything. I wanted it to be special, too. And I know you love dogs and dolphins, so I drew them just for you."

"They're great… I really don't want to go, Red," she says, and starts crying.

My eyes are burning. Not knowing what to say, I put my hand on her shoulder. The card slips off her lap and falls onto the deck of the bridge. My hand drops. Neither of us picks up the card.

"I got you something." Lacey reaches into her pocket and takes out a keychain. "A soccer ball," she says, and hands it to me. "I thought of you when I first saw it the other day. I asked my dad to buy it for you. Do you like it?"

The soccer ball is a see-through blue, all sparkly under the light. "It's real nice, Lacey." I force a smile. The snot in my nose wants to leak out, but I keep breathing it in. I pick up the card.

"I like you, Red," she says. "I always have."

A glass door slides open. There's Lacey's mother, standing in the doorway, shouting, "Lacey! Come back inside!"

I give her back the card. "It's time," I tell her.

Lacey gets off the rail. Before I do the same, she turns and kisses me on the cheek, near the lips. Looking up at her, I see she's about to cry again.

"Bye, Red," she says, and runs off with the card, not looking back.

I walk off the bridge toward the alleyway, feeling my heart break into pieces. I'm about two or three steps away from reaching the alleyway when suddenly I stop and turn around. Lacey. She's there, behind the closed balcony door, waving goodbye.

43

I did it. I'm here," he says, coming to a standstill at a three-way intersection. The Emerald Park block is facing him on the opposite side. Some of the townhouses are just as he remembers them, while others have been renovated to varying degrees. Propelling his cart forward, he crosses the street without checking for incoming cars and steps onto the sidewalk, his heart beating like a drum. No one's there, ahead of him, and most of the driveways here, on Sunny Street, are still empty. Anxiously he enters an alleyway, the wheels of his cart crunching on stone dust. As he approaches the other end, he can see more of that special place—a section of grass, the base of a mound, the shadow of a tree, gilded leaves—and his hands start to sweat a little on the handle. For so many years he never once thought about coming back for a visit. Why, so much has changed, he tells himself as he enters the park where the stone dust path turns into concrete. Instead of cutting through the green, he sticks to the concrete path, advancing slowly, trying to take in as much as he can, and to remember. The bridge is still there, waiting for him, beckoning to him.

The rest isn't the same. More trees, more bushes, he thinks. Less space. The main mound had nothing but grass when he moved away to another neighbourhood. Now there's a big rock where the soccer ball once was, with smaller rocks encircling it like a wreath. On one side of the park stood two maple trees that served as goal posts for soccer games. Now a small honey locust thrives in the goal area, forming with the posts an obtuse triangle. With all of these changes, he wonders if the children around here play anything at all, and have any of them even heard of kick-the-can?

So far he's been moving in a straight line with his cart, but now he's at a point where the concrete path turns into stone dust and winds like a snake through the park. To his relief the balconies are deserted, the sliding doors are closed with not a soul behind them looking on. The thought of having the park all to himself makes him want to stay a little longer. He's eager to step on that memorable bridge, to sit on it for old times' sake.

The flat-stone mound is to his left, the rock in its centre surrounded by geraniums in full bloom. Those boys—there were two of them—would've plucked the flowers out and made a bouquet for their mothers. What were their names? Alf? Alf and…? He doesn't remember. But he knows they were often together, like twin brothers. He gazes to the right at grassy areas still bare of trees, where he used to fight with boys much older than he, where he'd lie down on his back and watch the storm clouds float by, waiting for the first raindrops to fall.

The main mound is up ahead. He erases the big rock and imagines a soccer ball in its place. He imagines Lacey and

Mickey and a few others running up to the ball and laughing, running toward him as he walks on, running away from him on the path, across the grass, then vanishing in an instant. When he reaches the bushes near the bridge, he brings his cart to a halt. He lets his hand brush the upper leaves and finds his Lacey crouched there in the bushes, staring at him with her chocolate eyes. Stepping off the path, he walks straight to the main mound and places his hand on the rock. Everything around him—from the trees and bushes to the townhouses, the mounds, the bridge—everything looks so much smaller now that he's taller, now that he's back here.

He walks down the main mound and heads straight for the bridge, hearing the leaves rustle. Lacey's already seated on the rail, looking down at him as he approaches, her feet swinging back and forth to the beat of his footsteps. When he gets to the deck of the bridge, she's gone. He sits there, alone on the rail, feeling the texture of the wood and the breeze kissing his face, ruffling his hair. It's so small, he thinks. The bridge is so small he fears the whole deck will crumble under his weight. Just as he's about to get up, his eight-year-old self stops him. The boy's features are unmistakable: the short brown hair his mother would cut to save money; the eyes as dark as tree trunks; the nose still small, not fully developed. He's sitting on the rail opposite the beggar, and lodged between his feet is a soccer ball.

More flashes of the past come back to him in the stillness of this exceptional moment. He remembers some of the fights now, the frequent name-calling. He remembers that world of immaturity and inexperience, the hurt, the tears, the anger. But despite all of it he wishes more than anything to go back. To be the child he once was. To live forever in this place, this park, his home—if not forever, then to live and die here, without ever having to grow old. More than anything, he would choose the games he and his friends used to play; he would choose Lacey and Mickey, the alleyways, and his bike; he would choose Emerald Park over his life on the road.

Somewhere nearby, a sliding door opens. Children's voices reach him. He gets up and walks back to his cart beside the bushes. His first instinct is to leave the park immediately, but doing so would defeat the purpose of his visit. There's something he needs to do, something he needs to take.

He makes his way to the other side of the bushes and kneels on the grass, his hands touching the soil. If memory serves, it was buried right about there, between this bush and that one. Nervously the beggar looks over his shoulder for signs of movement or suspicious stares. Relieved at finding neither, he turns his gaze back to the soil and starts digging. He can feel the earth collecting under his nails and the beat of his heart quickening. When the hole is deep enough, he still doesn't see it. But where is it? he asks himself. He targets the spot on the left side of the hole and plunges his hands into the earth. It doesn't take long before something metallic appears. At first all he sees is a spot of pink, but as he digs and digs, his eyes catch a blue wave, a yellow heart, an orange diamond. He unearths the box and brings it to his lap, wiping off bits of dirt along the edges. He shakes it a little and hears something moving inside.

On opening it he's greeted by a keychain, a purple bunny sparkling like crystal. Under it are two sheets of folded paper and a lead pencil. The beggar pulls out a sheet and unfolds it. He recognizes the handwriting instantly, trying not to laugh at the sentence Lacey wrote in her own words so long ago: *I have*

a berth scarre on my but. He unfolds the other sheet and recognizes his own immature handwriting. The sentence reads:
I want my ma to be happy. With a faint, nostalgic smile, the
beggar looks back down at the box. There's one last item, an
unsealed envelope with his name written by an adult hand on
its front. He opens it curiously and takes out two sheets of
floral writing paper. He hears children laughing nearby, but he
doesn't look up. Putting all distractions aside, he focuses his
attention on the inked pages. Each word, each letter beckoning
to him like a luminous hand waving in the dark.

My dearest Red,

*I'm here, in the park where we first met, where
it all began. I'm sitting on the flat-stone mound,
relishing the view as I write. It's nice to be back.
To feel like a child again on this splendid day in
June. Emerald Park looks a bit different now
but it's still breathtaking, still unlike any other
park I've ever been to. Very soon I'll be heading
over to the bushes near the bridge. Of course if
you're reading this letter then you remember—
you remember our secret spot under the earth, the
only place I can communicate with you.*

*I'm on vacation for three weeks. To be honest, I
haven't been to Willobrooks since we last saw each
other two years ago. As much as I wanted to see
my parents, I wanted to see you more, to catch up
on lost time. I thought you were still living in the*

same apartment near the canal. When I got there I rang your buzzer downstairs, but someone else answered and so I left. I even went back to our bar, to your school, hoping you'd be there.

Memories. That's all I have of you—that and your ankle bracelet. I can't begin to describe how much I loved being with you, how special our time was. The hike on Mount Ashmore (which you didn't particularly like), our secret telephone calls when Cara wasn't home. Our restaurant dates downtown, the Old Port at sunset. And the lake. We could've had more, so much more had I kept my promise. I don't know if I'll ever forgive myself for pushing you away, for giving you false hopes. The fault is mine, not yours. I'm sorry for this. I truly am.

At the drive-in, when I told you I wanted to move here and be with you, I meant it. On the plane back to New York I thought about our future together, about finding a job in Willobrooks, being close to old friends and family. I thought it would be easy to leave my home for another, but I was wrong. For all sorts of reasons, life in New York got the upper hand. The truth is that it's always easier to say things than to do them. You get so caught up in your own bubble that you forget what was golden, you forget those moments of rapture that made you feel alive.

I miss you. I miss our talks—us. I hope you're all right. Maybe you moved on, and if you did I respect that. You'll probably never read this letter, but if you do then the past still means something to you.

I want you to know that I've always loved you. At seven I was too shy to tell you that. You took care of me, protected me, stood up for me when no one else did. I'd think about you during the day, asking myself if I'd see you later in the park, always hoping. Those summers were my favourites. I'd look forward to them because I knew you'd be there. I'm glad you were. In a way I wish I didn't have to write this letter. If only I could tell you everything in person, apologize to you in person.

No matter what, I'll always be your Lacey—I'll always be that little girl sitting on the bridge, lying on the grass facing the sky, kneeling under the kissing tree waiting for you. Just think of her and she'll be there with you, holding your hand.

Love always,

Lacey

His hands are trembling, and so is the letter. He looks up now, his eyes filled with tears, and turns his gaze to the main mound, where his eight-year-old self is counting with the soccer ball under his shoe. He puts the letter on the cover and grabs the pencil. There's enough room below Lacey's signature for a short message. The pencil is trembling as he writes.

> *Lacey,*
> *Thank you for the letter.*
> *You are every thing to me.*
> *I love you. Sorrey, my misstakes.*
> *Red*

Sniffling, he puts everything back into the box, including the keychain he initially wanted to take. After a brief moment of hesitation, he places the box in the hole before him and covers it with the earth. "There," he whispers, tapping the earth to make it flat again. "It's *our* little secret." The beggar turns around and sits on the grass, still sniffling. Looking to his left, he sees a boy and a girl with toys in their hands and dolls at their feet, playing on the deck of the bridge.

Acknowledgments

Many thanks to:

My best friend and amazing mentor, Jeff Loubier, for his precious input and constant support throughout my writing journey.

My talented friend Tristan Young, for his expert guidance on several key aspects of this book.

My top-notch illustrator, Michael Rehder, for his marvellous depiction of Emerald Park.

My superb editors, Lindsey Alexander, Michelle Meade, and Dan Varrette. Working with them has made me into a better writer, and for that I'm very, very grateful.

My family—above all, my loving parents—for always believing in me.